THE RED CLOAK

The Red Cloak

by

Dana Pride

Everlasting Publishing
Vancouver, Washington
USA

The Red Cloak
by
Dana Pride

Library of Congress Control Number
2010921745

ISBN: 0-9824844-7-X
ISBN 13: 978-0-9824844-7-0

First Edition
Everlasting Publishing
P.O. Box 965
Vancouver, WA 98666-0965
USA

*Although this book is fictional, it was inspired
by a real dream. God gave me the dream.
I just put it to paper.*

Dedicated to my family:
My husband, the Rev. Willie Pride; Mom and Dad; my brother, Dale; our daughter, Jahla; our son, Nathan; Mother Florence, Doreen, John, Delano, Virgil, Willie, Valesia, Akiia, Dawn, our grandchildren and our great-grandchildren. I love you all.

Dana

THE RED CLOAK

CHAPTER 1

Leeza Hamilton took a deep breath to clear her mind before going on stage. Too many things were trying to pressure her. She couldn't be thinking of any of them now; she had to be ready for her performance. Now was the time to fill her mind with positive thoughts.

She loved her job. She loved to perform. She loved her life. She had a wonderful man in her life. She had enough money so that it wasn't a worry for her, not even to worry about the ones who were trying to steal it from her. She had been given an opportunity to do what she loved to do, and she was doing it. She could do whatever she wanted to do, whenever she wanted to do it. She had millions of fans who loved her, who adored her, who wanted to be her. Her name was a household word.

She tuned in to the activity on stage. The previous act was finished and she was being introduced. She put on her wide smile, her stage smile, and let the feelings of power and joy propel her as she ran energetically onto the stage.

She was greeted by a roar of cheering as she grabbed the microphone – she didn't like using the headset mic. A microphone in her hand felt like a power tool, charging her and boosting her level of energy to its highest possible point. She was in charge of the performance now. She drew more and more force from the audience as she sang, hitting the high notes and extending the low notes. She could feel all eyes upon her; she could feel someone praying for her.

Where did that come from? No, she couldn't let herself be distracted! She had to concentrate. Everyone, from Jack-boy, her manager, to Chad Manager, her boyfriend, to the thousands of people in the audience tonight, expected perfection from her. Had she ever treated them to anything less than perfect? No, she had not, and she wasn't about to start now.

She finished her first song and drank in the applause and adoration. She was exhilarated! She loved nothing more than the feeling she got from the audience when she was on stage, when they showed her how much they loved her.

"Ham! Ham! Ham! Ham! Ham! Ham! Ham! Ham! Ham! Ham!!!" the audience shouted. She preferred when they shouted "Leeza" instead of "Ham," but she knew they were cheering for her with love, and they were not making sport of her.

"How are we doing tonight?" she asked the audience. She was answered by another roar of the crowd as she again gave them her wide stage smile. She could feel a rush of air on her molars. Yes, this was her wide smile. She was giving her best to her fans.

"Now it's time for one of my new songs. I don't know if you have heard this one yet, but it's coming to radio stations all over the country. Listen to the words – but get the meaning from my feelings." She waited for the music to start, and she caught the beat. She began to dance, further exciting the crowd. She began to sing.

"The words don't have a meaning
So listen to my feelings.
The words don't have a meaning
When you're talking about my heart.

You say that you'll come by today
I hear every word you say
You make a promise then walk away
Well, I don't believe you anyway.

The words don't have a meaning
So listen to my feelings.
The words don't have a meaning
When you're talking about my heart."

As she sang, she floated up into the air, outside her body, and observed herself performing while she watched from the highest pillar in the stadium, just below the clouds. She was entranced as she noted the beauty of her own movements, the perfection of her pitch, the quality of her voice pronouncing the words of the song. Her enunciation was excellent! Her dance moves were inventive, graceful, awe-inspiring. She had not seen such a performer as herself. She was amazed, as she seemed to be viewing a video of herself and the band in their greatest performance ever.

She automatically ran through the songs, one after another, without any variation, without any personal input. As the final song came to a close, she returned to her body like a genie returning to a bottle – slowly but precisely to the exact spot she left nearly 90 minutes ago. She again felt the rush of the crowd – she again could feel herself in her own body. She took a graceful bow before the audience as they cheered, louder and louder. This was what she loved! This was why she was alive, so she could receive this type of love from thousands of fans at one time! She gave her all to them, wrote songs they memorized and repeated, and they responded in love, in great numbers and with great force!

The concert ended and Leeza was ushered backstage. She went into her dressing room amid cheers and praises and flopped down in the chair in front of the mirror. She noticed that her face was covered with perspiration, her hair drenched. She didn't look as good in the mirror as she had from outside her body... she looked stressed, tired, worn. She recalled, not so long ago, when she would return to her dressing room super-charged, looking great, and ready to go to the party.

What was the point of her life? Was it merely to get a high from an adoring crowd, which quickly faded? The thrill she had received this evening had already dissolved. She glanced at the stack of this month's magazines on the table beside her, all of which featured her face on the cover. Wasn't this all she ever wanted? Was this all there was to life? She had attained her life goal at a young age... now what?

"Leeza, you were excellent, as usual," her manager, Jack-boy, said as he entered her dressing room without knocking.

"Jack, please knock!" she insisted.

"Knock, knock, Baby," he said. Jack-boy never took her seriously. "Wonderful show tonight. Sold out! Besides an excellent performance – have you ever been better? – an excellent total."

He always said that, 'an excellent total.' That phrase had lost its meaning with her.

"Let's do a free concert in the park," she suggested.

"Yeah, right," he laughed. "Are you crazy? Do you know how much moolah you'd be throwing away if you did a free concert?"

She hated it when he said 'moolah.'

"Why is it always about the money?"

"Oh, come on, Baby, don't go all hippie on me," he begged. "You have a huge staff to pay, you have a huge household to keep running, you need lots of moolah to maintain your daily lifestyle. You know that." He examined his face in the mirror.

"A concert in the park would be fun."

"A free concert in the park would be stupid." He scratched his head, and the sound of his fingertips against his scalp grated down her spine. Why was it so loud? Was he intentionally trying to bother her?

"Can you go now? I need to be alone."

"Come on, time for the party!"

"I don't want to go. I just want to be alone for awhile."

"Come on! You can be alone any other time! You are expected at the party! But get a shower first, you want to look your best."

"Are you saying I don't look my best?" Leeza frowned.

"I'm just saying you look like you need a shower."

"Thanks." She frowned at herself in the mirror.

"What's a manager for? Hey, where's Chad?" Jack-boy asked.

"Who knows?"

"Well, I don't know, that's why I asked you. Isn't he going to the party with you?"

"He said he'd be there, I don't know if he's here."

"Well, your limo is ready when you are. You gonna sign autographs tonight?" He looked in the mirror and groomed his hair.

"I have to, don't I? Yeah, I don't want to let down the fans in my own hometown." Leeza smiled.

"That's a good one! 'Hollywood – my own hometown.' Hey, that could be the title of your next album."

"Hey! I live here. It's my hometown."

"Yeah, right, small town girl from Hollywood. Get changed, and let's get going."

"As soon as you get going, I'm going to shower and change."

"Okay, okay, do you need any help?" He headed for the door. "Your assistants are just outside, waiting for you to call on them."

"I can shower and change by myself! But you can send Nita to get me a Starbucks. She knows which one to get."

"Ahhh, coffee of the week, eh? Sure, yeah, anything you want."

"Well, go! I want that coffee!" She pointed to the door.

"I'm gone!"

"I still see you!"

"I'm outta here," he said, slipping out of the dressing room. Leeza could hear the crowd of people outside her dressing room door as Jack-boy held them back, away from her. She got up from the chair and locked the door. She didn't need any help and she didn't need any interruptions.

Normally, she would have at least one assistant, probably Nita; she was her favorite, in her dressing room with her after a show. Leeza would be full of conversation and Nita would always respond appropriately, letting Leeza talk all she wanted, encouraging her, helping her, setting out her party attire, cleaning up after her. Tonight, Leeza didn't feel like talking. Her life was so wonderful, yet she felt so empty. Even Karman's constant flattery wasn't what she needed tonight. She needed a chunk of meaning, right now! It didn't have to last forever, she didn't have to be full of it, she just needed something to tell her she was important, her life did have meaning, she was more than a poster on a wall or a voice on a best-selling record or a face that sold magazines. She looked up at the ceiling.

"God, are you there?" she asked aloud. She slightly chuckled to herself. If He were there, was she expecting an answer from Him? She had never before called on Him, why would He be there for her? Wait; a long time ago, she had called on Him, years ago, as a teenager... she had asked Him for this, for this lifestyle, for this success. Was He the One who had given it to her, or had she done it herself? Maybe He did answer prayers.

"God?" she began again. "I know you are there. Does my life have a meaning? What's it all about? I have a lot, I mean, You have given me a lot... but I need more. Not more stuff, not more money, not more friends, but something else, something deeper. I need meaning in my life, meaning to my life, do you know what I mean?"

Of course He knew what she meant. He knew everything!

She threw her wet clothes on the floor and got in the shower. As she let the hot water relieve some of her tension, she began to feel better. She decided not to wash her hair – that would add another hour while she waited for Karman or Kelly to fix her hair. Well, it was all wet anyway, she needed to wash it, her scalp would start itching and stinking if she let this sweat sit in it any longer. She wasn't into wigs – maybe she could wear one of her high-fashion scarves.

She got out of the shower – she was burning up! – and looked through the outfits she had hanging in the closet. Each one made her look good – but tonight she didn't want to look too hot. She just wanted to look stylish, yet subtle. Did any of her clothes say that? Oh, yes, here was a gray flannel outfit she had never worn, sexy yet unobtrusive. She got dressed without any assistance and then unlocked the door. She opened it just the tiniest crack.

"Karman!" she called, then she shut the door.

In an instant, Karman was inside the dressing room with her.

"Leeza, you were fabulous tonight!" Karman said.

"Thanks, Karma," Leeza said, sitting in the chair in front of the mirror. "Do my hair – but just for a scarf, not all that."

"Okay… um… it's Karman, not Karma," she said tentatively.

"Yeah, I know, but what do you think about Karma?"

"You mean as a name, or as… karma?"

"Either one, what do you think?"

"I never thought about it." She gently pulled Leeza's hair into place.

"Well, think about it! You have a brain, don't you?"

"Leeza, you're so funny! Of course I have a brain! Everyone has a brain. I mean, how could I live without a brain?" she asked, as she combed the tangles from Leeza's hair.

"So… what's the meaning of life?" Leeza might as well ask. Maybe someone knew the answer, maybe even simple Karman.

"The meaning of life…" Karman said thoughtfully. "That's a good one. I give up. What is the meaning of life?"

"It's not a joke. I want your opinion, your take on this."

"The meaning of life…"

"Yeah, the meaning of life. Why are we here? What are we doing? What is the importance of our lives?"

"Well, it's different for you and me. For you, it's to make millions of people happy. For me, it's to make you happy."

"I don't mean the meaning of our jobs, I mean the meaning of our lives."

"Aren't we defined by what we do? Or who we are?"

Leeza didn't know how to answer that. She knew what she did, but she didn't know who she was, besides just being the famous Leeza Hamilton. What was the meaning of that?

CHAPTER 2

Leeza and her entourage rode in her limousine to the party, this one held at the home of one of the record producers. Everyone in the limo laughed and joked all the way there, with Leeza receiving the usual compliments on her excellent performance. They arrived in high spirits, making a commotion as they entered and greeted all the other people, famous, wanna-be famous, used-to-be famous, and married or dating famous. Leeza knew most of the people there and posed correctly as each one welcomed her and praised her. She smiled, hugged and allowed the greeting kisses as was expected of her, but she was feeling rather troubled. She thought about how Jack-boy often told her not to think too much, saying that she sometimes tried to over-analyze things, but she had no way to stop her mind from moving, and now it was moving in a single direction: to discover, or at least learn a little about, the meaning of her life.

"Leeza, Leeza, Leeza!" an older lady said, imitating the voice of a teenager, bringing Leeza back to the party. Leeza did not recognize her. She had a huge, toothy smile and wild, bright red hair. Leeza cringed at the color.

"Yes?" she asked tentatively. She hoped she wasn't about to be pulled into some boring conversation.

"Don't you remember me?" she asked. She reminded Leeza of one the characters in a Dr. Seuss book, but she couldn't recall which one.

"I am just so–" Leeza began.

"Oh, you remember!" the lady said, beginning to frown. She was much less attractive when she frowned, so Leeza hoped she could either get her to smile, or get away from her.

"I'm still flying high from the performance," Leeza said, "so you'll have to forgive me. My mind has not yet had a chance to catch up with me," she explained.

"Oh, yes, of course! You performed tonight!" she said enthusiastically. Fortunately, her smile returned to her sagging face.

Leeza wanted to remind her that this was the reason for the party, but she decided to let it go. She didn't want to prolong their exchange any longer than necessary. She gave the lady her wide smile.

"Well, I'm sure you were absolutely magnificent!" the lady exclaimed.

"Thank you very much for those kind words," Leeza said, desperate to escape.

"You know, you are really great," the lady continued, grabbing Leeza's hand. "What you have done for this country and for the environment are to be commended. You should get a medal!"

Now Leeza knew this lady did not know who she was. She had mistaken Leeza for somebody else, and Leeza could not think of a polite way to tell her. She was well trained to be very polite at these parties. She could never tell if the person was someone who could do great things for her career, or a reporter or gossip who could destroy her career.

"You know, I was just telling my husband, we should host a banquet in your honor. You know my husband; he always wants to do things on a grand scale. I mean, he can't ever do anything quietly or without being seen. He is such a character, and he wants to do something great, I mean, really big, I mean, huge, do you know what I mean? I mean, really, really big. He wants to get together all the big guys, with their checkbooks, of course, and have a fundraiser. Wouldn't that just about blow everything out of the water? I mean, something like this could put your financial goals for the organization over the top! And with your name attached, everyone would know who you are! And think of all the people who could be helped! This would definitely be a win-win, you know? Are you with me? What do you think about it? Do you have any thoughts? Of course, we would get your input. We would have to ask you – I mean, we couldn't do anything, even, without your permission. Don't even think we wouldn't ask you. So what do you think about the location? I mean, if we had it at our house, we would have to limit to about a hundred guests, but what do you think about the new plaza? I know they haven't opened yet, but my husband has connections. That does not need to be a worry of yours, my dear. You can just relax and know that we have everything in order. Not one worry should you have, not even about the tiniest little detail. You just leave it all to Boozie and me, we will do everything. All you have to do is show up! You won't have to perform or anything – but if you want to, we can work you into the program. So what do you think? Doesn't that sound like a winner? I mean to say, how can we lose? This would be just what we all need. Don't you agree?"

Leeza still had no idea who this lady was, or what she was saying. Her words were so bountiful, they were meaningless, just flooding out of her mouth and overflowing Leeza's mind without any significance. Leeza doubted that the lady even knew what she was saying... and what kind of name was Boozie, anyway?

"Leeza!" somebody shouted, coming to her rescue. She excused herself from this woman and turned toward the voice, which was coming from a very animated Jack-boy.

"Leeza, you have to be careful," he whispered into her ear, as he quickly pulled her away from this lady.

"I always am," Leeza assured him. "You know my motto: be careful or die."

"Forget about that now. Do you know who she is?" he asked.

She shook her head. "Should I?"

"I'm thankful you don't!" he said, relieved. "She is the witch of Beverly Hills!"

"Is she a good witch, or a bad witch?" Leeza asked.

"No, I'm serious! She does black magic, casts spells on people and stuff." He looked like he really was serious.

"I don't believe in all that," she told him.

"Well, you better start!" he warned. "She has been responsible for some really odd happenings."

"Odd happenings? Like what?"

"Like, she made Charles Shramshrock think he was a horse."

"What? She couldn't do that." Leeza smiled at the thought.

"She did! For days, all he would do was eat grass and whinny, and trot around his house."

"I don't believe in that."

"Demons are at work here! Don't you see what I'm saying?"

"Demons, witches, werewolves, vampires, they don't have any power over me. I don't believe in them. I love God, and He is stronger than anyone – especially fictional characters."

"Leeza, you've got to watch out–"

"Jack-boy!" golden-haired Chad called. "So you're the one who's been hiding my baby! Hello, my Cupcake," he said to Leeza. He moved in smoothly and gave her a kiss. "I've been looking for you. You know I have to go to New York tonight, right? Want to ride to the airport with me?"

"When do you have to go?" she asked. She wanted to have a nice conversation with him, and to let him rub the tension out of her shoulders, and tell her everything was all right. He was so good-looking, he put all other male models to shame. Leeza, and every other female, for that matter, was content to just stare at his handsome features, his naturally wavy, beautiful hair, his sensitive, knowing, deep blue eyes.

"In a few minutes," he said.

"Can I just go with you to New York?" she asked, knowing that she couldn't go.

"Oh, yeah, and make my dreams come true," he said, gently resting his hands on her upper arms. "I wish you could come with me."

"Yeah, me too. I would love to ride with you to the airport, but I just got here and I really should stay here awhile," she said.

"It's your party, you can leave if you want to," he sang. "Then you could come back."

"How would that look, if I left my own party, and then came back?" she asked. "Once I go, I have to be gone for good."

"Absolutely. You must follow the protocol."

"I'm going to miss you."

"I'll call you three times a day." He touched her lips.

"I'll answer you three times a day." She kissed his finger.

"Keep your cell phone with you at all times."

"You know I will. I couldn't stand it if I missed a call from you." She looked deeply into his enchanting blue eyes.

"Me, either. Or is it 'me, neither'? Either way, like-same."

"Is this a private party?" Lance Shuman, one of Chad's assistants asked, as he put his arms around the two of them, giving them both a hug. "Leeza, you look fabulous. You are really over the top tonight. And Chadly, the limo is waiting for you."

"I know, I know," Chad said, while looking directly into Leeza's eyes.

"The limo will wait, but the plane won't," Lance said.

"There will be another one," Chad said, mesmerizing Leeza with his beautiful, staring eyes.

"Not until tomorrow, and you have that early morning shoot. Remember, they're on East Coast time, four hours ahead."

"And I am on Leeza's time," Chad said, holding both of her hands, kissing them.

"Yeah, but you don't have a four million dollar contract with her, waiting for you in the morning."

"She's worth more than money to me."

"Chad," Leeza began. He put his finger to her lips.

"Only one more minute, one more kiss," he said, kissing her gently, until Lance separated them.

"Now, Chadderson," Lance said, pulling on his arm.

"Hey! Watch the merchandise!" Chad said. He was very sensitive about his body – and with good reason. His fortune depended on it. "I have a swim suit shoot tomorrow. I can't have any marks on the skin!"

"Yeah, yeah, let's go," Lance said impatiently.

"But I can have one more mark on the lips," he said, turning to Leeza, giving her one last kiss. He then stepped back slowly, one step at a time, watching her as he walked to the door while Lance made sure he didn't bump into anyone. "Goodbye, my love." He blew her a kiss.

"Chad," Leeza said softly, "I love you." She waved a tiny wave.

"Until next week, when we meet again, my love," he said, as Lance opened the door for him.

"Catch ya later, Leeza," Lance said, spoiling the romance of the moment.

Leeza stood watching the door for a moment, thinking about how unfair it was that she was able to spend so little time with the one she loved. She now was alone in the crowd, expected to be so chipper, so ready with a smile, when she just didn't feel like being here any more. Chad had taken with him the little amount of joy she had felt in her heart. She didn't see anyone here who sparked her interest; they were all in their own little circles, their own little, meaningless worlds. Chad was important to her, but what did that mean, when they couldn't be together? She took a step towards the door, but a group of people stepped in front of her, blocking her way.

"Leeza, darling," one of the wives said, taking both of her hands and looking straight into her eyes. She swayed to the left and right, then steadied herself, as if she were about to say something. She opened and closed her mouth several times, like a fish.

Leeza could see she was intoxicated, and she didn't have much tolerance for people who were under the influence of alcohol or drugs. She smiled, looking for someone to come to her rescue. Where had Jack-boy gone? He was usually right with her, protecting her from people and situations like this.

"Excuse me, please," Leeza said, stepping away from the lady as she searched for someone she who could hold a real conversation with her. Why had her entourage dispersed after the introductions had been made? Where were the ones who were usually close to her? She looked at this group that was crowded into this huge house, all somewhat familiar to her, as if they were extras from all the movies. She seemed to know most of them by face, but she didn't see anyone she knew well enough to approach. She felt herself rise above this collection of extras, listening to the general buzz or roar, unable to understand anything anybody was saying distinctly. This party was happening to celebrate her performance, her status, but she felt as if she were merely a bystander, or a reporter, an intruder. She was just feeling out of place, out of sorts... out of her mind?

She told herself she should be happy, thankful, that all this was arranged for her, that she had such a great life, and that so many people loved her. However, was this how they thanked her, by getting drunk and taking all kinds of expensive drugs, putting on airs, and acting foolish? Somebody lit a cigarette in the room – didn't everyone know she hated that smell, that she was sensitive to even the smallest amount of smoke in the air? Why wasn't anyone telling that person to extinguish that awful cancer stick? She knew what would happen next: someone else would think smoking was allowed here, and in just a few minutes, the room would be filled with smoke, her eyes would be burning and she would begin to cough. She couldn't risk damaging her throat. Her career depended on her voice, and her staff depended on her career.

Leeza decided she had had enough of the party. Uncharacteristically for her, without saying goodbye to anyone – usually she made an exit as grand as her entrance, touching bases with all the notable attendees on her way to the door – she slipped out the front door unnoticed. Dennis was leaning against the limo, listening to his iPod. He stood up straight and pulled out his ear buds when he saw her coming towards the car.

"Is everything alright?" he asked, opening the door for her.

"Yeah, I just wanna leave now," she answered, climbing into the back seat.

"Alone? I mean, no one is going with you?"

"Not this time. Hey, Denny, can we just drive for a while? I don't feel like going home right now. I just want to get away from here."

"Whatever is your pleasure, my dear Leeza. Do you have a preference – a destination in mind?"

"Let's go north. Drive up the coastline, north."

Dennis closed her door and went around to the driver's side. "Would you like to listen to some music?" he asked, as he got in the car.

"No, I just want to think. But keep the window open, I want to ask you something."

"Go right ahead." He started the engine and began to drive. They drove in silence for a while before Leeza spoke. "What does it all mean? I mean, what is the meaning of life?"

"You mean, like, life, liberty and the pursuit of happiness?"

"No, not some cliché – why are we here?" She looked out her window, as if they might be passing by the answer.

"We're here because you asked me to drive north."

"No, I mean, here, alive; what is the meaning of life?"

"Well, for me, to provide for my family, to enjoy what God has given me, to take care of your driving needs and this car..." Dennis turned onto the highway.

"Isn't there more than that?"

"For you, sure! You have everything! You can make life just what you want it to be."

"But I just don't know." Leeza shook her head.

"Darling, nobody knows – that is one of the mysteries of life. You can take a lifetime to discover the meaning of your life, or you can just enjoy it, one day at a time."

"Stop with the clichés!"

"Yes, ma'am."

"Sorry, I didn't mean to snap at you. I'm just going through a crisis right now." She stuck her lip out in a pout.

"Leeza, pardon me for speaking out... may I?"

"Yes, please. Just tell me what's on your mind."

"When a mother loses her only child to an illness, that is a crisis. When the doctors tell you there's nothing else they can do, that is a crisis. When a wife finds out her husband is on drugs or having an affair, that is a crisis. When a family can't afford to keep their home and they are put out on the street, THAT is a crisis. When your brother goes to jail for ten years, that's a crisis. What you are dealing with is not a crisis, it's only in your own mind. I think you are putting too much emphasis on your state of mind."

"A state of mind can be a crisis! Look at all the crazy people!"

"They might have a mental illness, or they are just doing it to themselves, like you are."

"What? Are you saying—"

"Look, Miss Drama Queen, I mean no disrespect, but you are making a mountain out of a molehill. You have everything anyone could want! But what about your soul?" He seemed to be genuinely interested.

"That's what I mean! What about my soul?" She nodded her head frantically.

"What about your soul?"

"What does it need?" She leaned forward to hear some great revelation.

"I think you need to go to church."

She snapped back into her seat. "Don't go all religious on me."

"If you're concerned about your soul, maybe you should go to church," he said, shrugging his shoulders.

"I connect with God in my own way."

"It seems like that isn't enough for you. You would be surprised what you could get out of going to church."

"Don't tell me what to do!" she shouted.

"I'm merely making a suggestion. You asked."

"Okay, I guess... hey! Pull off the freeway! Stop over there!"

"What? Where?"

"Over there. I want to walk down the beach, and feel the sand between my toes. This looks like a safe beach, doesn't it?"

"I don't see anyone around. Do you want me to walk with you?"

"No, I want to walk by myself. Just wait for me here."

CHAPTER 3

Leeza removed her shoes and got out of the car. The sun would be rising in a few minutes – the night was warm. She rushed down to the beach and enjoyed the loose sand between her toes. She went to the edge of the water and dipped her toes in it – brrr, the water was cold! She began to run, run, run! beside the water's edge, on the firm sand, making indentations that immediately disappeared.

She became suddenly aware that she was not alone. She stopped and looked around her, checking her surroundings. A hooded figure was approaching her. She did not need to be afraid. No one would harm the great, the famous Leeza Hamilton.

The person came closer to her. Leeza breathed deeply, wondering if this were a crisis. Should she run? She could probably move much more quickly than a person in a full-length cloak. The cloak drew her attention. In the early morning light, it began to reveal its color – it was red. She hated red! She was known for hating the color red! She had nothing to do with the color red! But here it was, coming straight at her, red, red, red! How could a person wear such an awful color so boldly? Who was this person?

She would have to kill this person and throw the cloak in the ocean! How could she do it? Should she try to drown him? Maybe she could hit him with a piece of driftwood. Her heart pounded. That red was really bothering her, as the color made itself known in the growing daylight. She was going out of her mind! She couldn't kill anyone! She had to let the red cloak exist! No, she had to let the person exist, and she had to dispose of that hideous red cloak.

She made up her mind to stand her ground and speak to this person, to insist that she be given the cloak immediately. She was formulating in her mind what to say – she didn't want to appear to be crazy – when the cloaked person stopped a few feet away from her. The moment became surreal; time slowed as Leeza peered into the hood and she stood looking at a familiar face. They stared at each other for a moment, examining each other.

"What do you want from me?" Leeza shouted.

"You are me," a voice answered.

"What?"

The figure pulled down the hood of the cloak to reveal a face that looked just like Leeza's – only without the makeup, without the stress lines, without the fancy hair surrounding it.

"You look just like me," the young lady said.

"No, you look just like me," Leeza insisted.

"Same difference."

"Who are you?" Leeza looked closely at her face.

"Jane."

"Just plain Jane?"

"Plain Jane, yeah, you can call me that. I guess to you I'm just a plain Jane." Jane looked away from her, toward the ocean.

"What are you doing here?"

"I live right up there." She pointed without looking.

"You live here?" Leeza asked, clearly impressed. What a beautiful place to make a home, right near the ocean! Why hadn't she thought of that?

"Jane, it's nice to meet you. I'm –"

"I know who you are. Everyone knows who you are. What are YOU doing here, on my beach?" Jane demanded.

"Is this a private beach? I'm sorry, I didn't know..."

"No, I don't mean as in 'private,' I mean, here, in my neck of the woods," Jane said apologetically.

"I just had to get away and I wanted to take a walk on the beach."

"You look really tired. Have you been up all night?"

"As a matter of fact, I have. I just did a concert last night, and then there was this party." Leeza threw her hands in the air to make her point.

"Ah, the lifestyles of the rich and famous. Well, it was nice meeting you. I have to get back home before my family wakes up."

"You have a family?"

"I live with my sister and my baby."

A life with a meaning stood before Leeza.

"Would you mind if I come to your house with you? Just for a minute, I mean? I don't want to bother you or anything, I was just wondering..."

"Sure, come on. Just be quiet when we get inside." Jane began to walk toward her house.

"Yeah, sure, I won't say a word... or I'll just whisper," Leeza said, as she followed Jane.

"That's the idea."

They climbed a flight of wooden stairs, which rose above the beach, and Leeza had the strongest feeling of déjà vu. This reminded her of a beach house she had visited as a child. The soothing sound of the ocean, the fresh scent in the air, the salty taste on her lips, took her back to the fringe of a memory – it slipped away just that fast, it was gone. The place was so familiar, yet so unknown. As she stepped into the house, she was enveloped by a warmth and comfort she hadn't experienced in a long time. She felt as if she had entered a home that had *meaning*. Jane took off the red cloak and put it on a hanger in the closet. Leeza was so relieved to get that loud, hideous color out of her sight! An idea began to formulate in her mind. She didn't have another show scheduled until Saturday... Maybe, just maybe, for one day she could disappear.

Jane led Leeza into the kitchen. Leeza began to ask Jane questions about her life, to learn as much as she could about her.

"What's your sister's name?"

"Sharla."

"What about your baby? Boy or girl? How old is it? What's its name? Can I see it? What do you do for a living?"

"IT is a girl and HER name is Shari. She is the most beautiful baby in the world." Jane opened the refrigerator door.

"Let's trade places," Leeza suggested.

"What?" Jane slammed the refrigerator door.

"Trade places, you and me. I need to get away. You won't have to do anything. Just have my driver, Dennis, take you to my house and you can stay there. Then tonight, have him bring you back." Leeza nodded her head in an effort to persuade her.

"I can't just leave my baby here with you. I don't know you."

"We'll be fine. I'll ask your sister what to do if I need help. How hard can it be, taking care of a baby?"

"I can't leave my baby," Jane said, shaking her head.

"Well, you can't take her. Here, let's change clothes. Come on, it will be fun. No one will ever know."

"How will I know what to say? Or what to do?"

"Just say whatever you want. You can do whatever you want. That's what I do." Leeza smiled.

"I'm not like you. I can't just do whatever I want."

"You can now! This is going to be great!"

"I can't do it. I can't leave my baby and go stay in your house."

"Just for one day. Later tonight, at night, we'll meet down on the beach, same place as we met this morning. I'll wear the red cloak and we can change places, you'll put on the cloak."

No one would ever guess Leeza would be wearing a red cloak; no one would recognize her. This was the perfect plan.

"Can't do it." Jane pursed her lips.

"Come on! I need a vacation!"

"Can't do it."

"Yes, you can! We can!" Leeza bobbed her head, then went over to the sink. She turned on the water and tore a paper towel off the roll.

"If you need a vacation, just go to Hawaii or something," Jane said.

"No! Whenever I go anywhere, everyone knows me." She began scrubbing off her makeup with a damp paper towel. "Here, no one will know me. I'll be you. And you will be me."

"I wouldn't know what to do."

"You don't have to do anything! Just do whatever you want! Be me! If anyone asks you anything, just answer like you would normally answer." Leeza dried her face with another paper towel, trying not to notice how scratchy it felt on her delicate skin.

"I don't normally have a chef to cook my meals and a personal trainer to take me for a walk and a driver to drive me around. Nothing in your life would be normal to me."

"That's what would make this so great! If you don't feel like walking, just tell Gretchen you don't want to walk! You can tell Hans to fix anything you want to eat – he's the best! Or just tell him to surprise you and he'll make you something you'll never forget – low calorie and nutritious, with a taste that's out of this world. Or if you want to go anywhere, Dennis will take you, wherever you want to go."

"I don't want to go anywhere! I just want to stay here. Come on, I'll fix us some tea and then you can go back to your world and I'll stay here." Jane moved to the counter and pulled a teapot out of the cupboard.

Leeza was not satisfied with that answer. She was used to getting her way. No, she couldn't leave this home without having an opportunity to taste of its meaning, of the reason it was a home and not just a house. She had to convince Jane that trading places, just for a day, was the best option for both of them. She had to become Plain Jane, to live her life, to experience a life with a meaning.

"Can I ask you something?"

"Just don't ask me to trade places," Jane warned.

"No, I just want to know, what do you think is the meaning of life?"

"Wow, you really are messed up, aren't you?"

"What do you mean?"

"Hey, I can't go live your life and sleep with your boyfriend, and you are not going to stay here and sleep with mine."

"You have a boyfriend?"

"How do you think I got a baby?"

"What's his name?"

"I told you, she's a girl."

"No, I mean your boyfriend."

"Burton."

"Does he live with you?"

"No, he has his own apartment. Just Sharla, my sister, lives here with my baby, Shari, and me."

"Look, it's just for one day. Chad is out of town all week. You won't have to deal with him. If Burton calls or comes over, I'll just tell him I/you have a headache, and I need to be alone for a day or two." She reached for a picture on the mantle, a picture of a young man who looked strangely familiar to her. "Is this him? He's so cute! I can see why you don't want to lose him. I'll leave him alone, I promise."

"I just can't leave my baby. I just can't go."

Jane's life had meaning, with the baby. This wasn't a good enough reason to have a baby, though, but having one would add some meaning to a life.

"Let me see her. Come on, I'd be a good mother."

"Look, no offense, but what I've heard about you, you're selfish and self-centered, not really doing anything for anyone else."

"That is not true! I am very generous, and I take good care of my staff."

"I don't mean, like, buying things, I mean, like, being there, supporting them."

"I support more people than you probably know."

"That's not what I mean!"

"Well, if we trade places, even for a day, maybe I can learn something about what you're talking about, you know? And you can see what I do. Come on, where is the baby?"

"Quietly, let's go upstairs. Her room is at the top of the steps. I don't think she's awake yet."

The climbed the stairs and Leeza found herself looking at the most beautiful baby in the world. She had to stay here, and get acquainted with Jane's life. The baby was tiny and delicate, soft and pure. Leeza longed to pick her up and hold her – but she could do that later, after Jane left. She grabbed Jane's hand and led her back down to the kitchen.

"Come on, you have to let me stay here," Leeza begged.

"Why don't you just stay here with me?"

"No! If you don't go back in my place, people will start looking for me."

Somehow, after briefing Jane on everything she would need to know to become her, Leeza was able to convince Jane to trade places with her. Jane reluctantly agreed to exchange clothes, and exchange lives, just until tonight. As Leeza slipped out of her smart gray flannel suit, Jane gasped.

"You're not wearing any underwear!" she whispered loudly.

"I never do. It bugs me." She grabbed some of Jane's clothes.

"Well, while you're here, you need to wear some of mine. If my sister sees you without underwear, she's going to know you are not me. And while I'm you, I WILL be wearing my undergarments."

"No problem. No one will check. Okay, you need to go now and meet Dennis. He's waiting at the limo just down the beach and up the hill, in that public parking area. I'm pretty sure he'll be the only limo driver standing there. He'll take you to my house. When you get there, just open the door and walk in. Go up the stairs and you'll be in my room – my room is the entire third floor."

"Don't I need a key?"

"Never carry one. I hate to carry anything – too much stress to remember where stuff is. Dennis will let you in the house." She paused, hearing a noise. "What was that?"

"That's my sister getting up. Let me get out of here, or we'll have some explaining to do, and one thing my sister can't do is keep a secret," Jane said.

"Okay, 11:00 tonight, have Dennis bring you to the same parking lot again. I'll meet you at one in the morning at the same spot where we met, and I'll be wearing the red cloak. When we are sure no one is watching, I'll give you the cloak, and we'll both return to our own lives. Simple, isn't it?"

"It isn't, but it might be fun. Just for one day, that's it. Then we switch back. Right?" Jane said doubtfully.

"Do you doubt me? You said it, I am you. I can do anything you can do. It'll be a snap! You have nothing to worry about! Go, have a blast being me! We'll switch back tonight."

Jane slipped out the door as Leeza sat down at the kitchen table. This was going to be her best vacation ever!

CHAPTER 4

Leeza had just finished a cup of tea when Sharla came down the steps carrying Shari. Leeza suddenly had no idea what to do. She hadn't heard the baby make any noise! How was she to know she had awakened? Should she be doing something? She decided to follow Sharla's lead.

"Hey," Sharla said, putting Shari in the high chair.

"Hey," Leeza said, trying to sound like Jane.

"Pretty humid out on the beach today?"

"Um, yeah. I guess," Leeza answered, with no idea what Sharla was talking about,

"Your hair got a little wild out there."

"Oh, really? I didn't notice." How did Sharla notice? She hadn't even looked at Leeza.

"You never do."

"What do you mean by that?"

"Get off your high horse and come down to reality." She began feeding Shari baby food from a jar.

"Okay," Leeza said, not wanting to argue with this woman who thought she was her sister.

"Open up... good girl!" Sharla said, using a high voice. Shari opened her mouth wide. Sharla stuck some food in her mouth, Shari spit it out, Sharla scooped it off her face with the spoon and put it in her little mouth again.

"You're really good with her," Leeza said.

Sharla gave her a dirty look, then she continued feeding the baby. Leeza wondered when she would be taking over her motherly duties, but she was glad now to just have a lesson.

"Hi, Shari," she squeaked in a high voice. Shari stopped eating, looked at this odd stranger for a second, then she resumed focusing her attention on Sharla. Great, Leeza thought, I've fooled my own sister but not my own baby.

"What are you doing today?" Sharla asked.

Oh, what a tough question, and so early in the morning! "I don't know yet," Leeza answered.

"Come on, open up," Sharla said to Shari. All Leeza wanted to do was to observe Sharla take care of Shari, and learn about a life that had real meaning to it. They were fascinating to watch! Shari looked at Sharla expectantly, sometimes pounding one hand on the tray of her high chair – not out of frustration, but out of joy. Sharla smiled as she fed her, making faces, opening her mouth when she wanted Shari to open hers, and Shari was making the cutest little sounds. They could have been the only two people in the world – they were in their own world. Leeza didn't feel jealous; she felt ignorant. She had no idea this type of relationship between two people existed. She could be one of those people – she should be, at least for today, while she was Shari's mother. Leeza wasn't sure what to do right now, so she just kept watching, and kept quiet.

Sharla came out of the baby world for a moment, proving that she was part of the larger world, the real world, to speak to Leeza.

"You're so quiet this morning. Are you okay?" she asked.

"I've just been doing a lot of thinking," Leeza answered, entranced by the rhythm of the dip, shove, spit, scoop, shove routine.

"Well, it's about time," Sharla said. "You didn't strain a brain muscle or anything, did you?"

"Very funny," Leeza said, wondering if this was typical sister-sister talk. Didn't sisters have their own language, their own banter, their own special kind of conversation between them, a conversation with years of history behind it, years of familiarity and shared experiences? Leeza realized she was in a situation that was way out of her league, attempting to step into a life where she didn't have any of that. She was a performer, not an actress.

"Well, I'm going to go see Mom this morning," Sharla said, finishing the jar of baby food and wiping Shari's face.

"Mom?" Leeza said. She didn't know Jane's mother was still living! But why wouldn't she be? She probably wasn't that old. Leeza would like to go with Sharla, to meet her 'mother,' but she knew this wasn't the time to ask about it. She would do better to stay here and get familiar with her house and her baby.

"Yeah, Mom," Sharla said. "You do know who I mean, don't you? I mean, you are not that far out of it, are you? Did you take your medication this morning?"

"Of course," Leeza said, wondering what she meant. "I always do." She hoped that was the right answer, then she began to be curious about who this Plain Jane really was. She had a simple life, a quiet life, away from the spotlight and the crowds, but she was complicated. Why would a young girl like her need medication? Maybe that was why Sharla was taking authority with the baby, instead of just waiting for Shari's own mother to do it, because Jane needed some help, or she wasn't all there.

"Yeah, right," Sharla said. "I'm going to get ready now. Come on, Shari," she said, lifting her to her shoulder, on which she had placed a towel. She patted her back until Shari gave a cute little burp, then a second, louder one. "Good girl. Now it's time to play."

After Sharla put Shari in the playpen and went upstairs, Leeza quietly went over to the side of the playpen and looked at the baby. Shari truly was the most beautiful baby in the world! Her arms were so smooth and chubby, little wisps of curls covered her head, her little body sat there like a pug dog, a little chunk of a baby. For this whole day, Shari was her baby. Leeza should have paid closer attention to the food Sharla was giving her... but it didn't really matter. Whatever was in the cupboard must be the right kind. How would she know when to feed her? She didn't want to act like she didn't know anything about babies, after all, she was in the role of a mother now, but how was she going to learn anything about her, and how to take care of her?

She sat on the sofa beside the playpen and watched Shari play. She wondered how old she was – a question she didn't think of asking Jane when she was here, and she surely couldn't ask Sharla. Shari grabbed a little plastic toy with her chubby hand and pulled it to her mouth, which she opened wider than she had any time at breakfast. Leeza wanted to say something to her – Shari didn't even seem to be aware that she was there – but she didn't know what to say. She was content to just watch. Right now, she was learning more from this tiny person than she could ever learn on her 200+ channels of cable.

"Okay, I'm outta here," Sharla said, as she came down the steps. "Need anything while I'm out?"

"I can't think of anything," Leeza said.

"You can't think," Sharla said.

Leeza decided she must have been teasing. "Right now, I am concentrating on this baby. I am completely satisfied." She was telling the absolute truth.

"That's the most sensible thing you've said in a long time," Sharla said. "See ya."

"Bye."

CHAPTER 5

Leeza was alone in the house with Shari. She longed to hold her, but she didn't want to break her. Although the baby was chunky, she seemed so fragile, so trusting, as if she knew nothing bad could happen to her. Security, that's what she had. She was secure in her environment. Even though she seemed to be ignoring Leeza, she had not a worry in the world.

Leeza decided to explore the house. It was a fine-looking house, very small, compared to her house, but very beautiful, with natural wood walls and hardwood floor. Everything seemed to be right where it should be. The layout of the house was so logical; the placement of each item was so perfect for a house on the beach. Downstairs were the kitchen with an attached dining area and a pantry, a nice little living room, an office and a family room. She and Jane had entered through the kitchen door, where there was a little entry area which held shoes boots and towels and baskets and everything necessary for going down to the beach, and a little bathroom off to one side. Sharla had left through the front door, right beside the closet, which held the red cloak.

Leeza went upstairs. The natural wood made it seem a little dark inside the house, but it was so attractive and so well kept. She first came to Shari's room, small and filled with baby things: a white crib, a changing table, two little white dressers, and all sorts of decorations. There was also a day bed in the room. Leeza imagined that Jane rested there while Shari was taking her nap. She moved to the next bedroom.

This must be Sharla's room. Everything was neat and in place, and the room smelled like Sharla. This couldn't be Jane's room... how did she know? She just could tell. The furniture matched the wood of the walls. The bed was made, tight as a drum. Everything was in order, neat as a pin. She didn't have any pictures on the walls. Maybe this was a guest room?

As she opened the door to the next room, she stopped, stunned. This was her own bedroom! The only difference was the presence of red – the bedspread was red, the curtains were red, this was a room of red. However, the design and lack of neatness definitely made this her room. Clothes were strewn all over the place, the bed was unmade, posters covered the walls, and framed photographs cluttered the dresser. She picked up the photos, one at a time – Jane and Sharla, in the mountains, a few years ago; Sharla and Shari, close-up of their faces; Jane and Sharla as two little girls in blue Easter dresses... Mom. This was a photo of their mother, with kind eyes and a familiar smile, Jane's smile. Leeza studied it for a long time. She knew this woman... she had known this woman... had she been her teacher, in that long-ago world of school? No, she had been closer than a teacher... who was she?

A cry broke into her thoughts. The baby was downstairs alone! What was the matter with her? Leeza flew down the steps and leapt to the side of the playpen. Shari had tipped over and was lying on her side, chewing on a toy.

"What's the matter, Baby?" Leeza asked uncomfortably.

Shari ignored her.

"Do you want to sit up?"

Shari gave her no response.

"Can I pick you up?"

Shari continued to chew on her toy.

Leeza awkwardly reached into the playpen and tried to get a grip on the baby. Shari was like a huge lump of clay, without any handles, letting her manipulate her into position. Leeza propped her up so she was sitting, then placed her hands under her arms to lift her.

"Ahhhh!" Shari screamed, almost causing Leeza to drop her.

"It's okay, Baby," Leeza said, trying to imitate Sharla's baby-talk voice. She pulled her close to herself and felt the warmth radiating from her. This was a real baby! Leeza held her and hugged her, hoping this moment would never end. This was a life with meaning! Hugging a baby added meaning to life!

Shari gripped Leeza's hair and pulled it.

"OW!" Leeza shouted. That really hurt – but she couldn't get mad at Shari. She was just a baby and she didn't know what she was doing. Shari looked around the room, uninterested. Leeza loosened the baby fingers' grip on her hair and put her hair behind her back.

"We don't pull hair," she said, in her normal voice. Shari seemed to understand. Ahh, this was the way to talk to her, the same as she would to any person.

"Shari, I'm Leeza," she said. "I'm not your mommy, but I'm pretending to be her, just for now. You just treat me like you treat your mommy, and everything will be fine."

Shari looked right at Leeza, as if she understood. Then she smiled and made a funny face.

"You understand me, don't you?" she asked.

Shari's face turned bright red and she grunted. Leeza felt something moving, something warm, in the area where her lower hand was, near the baby's bottom. Shari smiled again.

"You messed your diaper!" Leeza exclaimed. When would Sharla be home? She might be gone for a long time. What was Leeza to do? Shari began to cry.

"It's okay, Baby, I'll take care of it." Leeza was smart. She could figure out how to change a diaper. She looked around the room for a clue, then she remembered the baby's room. She had a changing table!

Leeza zipped up the stairs with Shari in her arms. Shari must be terribly uncomfortable, with all that crying she was doing. Leeza rushed her to the changing table and gently – oh, so gently – laid her on her back. She looked around the room for what she needed... a diaper, something to use to wipe her... Shari cried and rolled to her side, just as Leeza turned to catch her before she fell off the changing table. Those little sides didn't seem like they would hold her. Leeza kept one hand on Shari, to hold her in place, and searched the room. Where would Jane keep the things she needed for changing her baby? Leeza calmed herself by breathing deeply. Ew, the stink of a dirty baby was unbearable!

Handy, she thought, they should be handy. Sure enough, a dispenser attached to the changing table held moist wipes, and under the table, on a shelf below the baby, were stacks of disposable diapers. Still keeping one hand on the baby, she pulled up a diaper and opened the package of wipes. Then she began to figure out how to remove the little outfit Shari was wearing... hmm, snaps. She successfully removed the diaper – oh, how terrible the smell was growing! Where was she to put it? She set it gently on the floor so the runny mess wouldn't spill out of it. She pulled out three wipes and began to clean the baby's little bottom. Three was not enough – she needed to use at least ten to finish the job. When she was satisfied that the baby was clean enough, Leeza began to maneuver the clean diaper into place. Why hadn't she ever played with dolls when she was a kid? Shari was wiggling her legs and the diaper wasn't staying where Leeza wanted it to be.

"I need a little cooperation here, Baby," she said. Shari stopped moving and looked right at Leeza's face.

"That's better," Leeza said, finally getting the diaper in the right place and then sealing it with the adhesive strips. "Good girl!"

Shari smiled at Leeza.

"We did it!" Leeza said, proud of her accomplishment.

Shari looked right at Leeza, laughed with abandon, and pooped again.

"What did you do that for?" Leeza asked, as if expecting an answer. Oh, well, now she was practiced at this. Changing the second diaper was much easier than the first. When she finally finished, with Shari happily watching her every move, Leeza set Shari in the crib so she could clean up the mess. This was really awful. Leeza normally had someone else to clean up after her, and now, here she was, cleaning up after a baby. However, it wasn't that bad. As a matter of fact, she kind of had a feeling of satisfaction of a necessary job well done.

She could have used a cup of coffee, but she hadn't seen any in the kitchen, nor did they have a coffee maker. She realized she had been awake all night and she felt kind of tired. Shari was sucking her thumb and beginning to doze, and the day bed looked very inviting. Leeza curled up with her head on a pillow and drifted off to sleep.

CHAPTER 6

Leeza awakened in a panic. She was supposed to be doing something, wasn't she? But what was it? Where was she? She blinked her eyes as the room began to become somewhat familiar. Yes, she was in a baby's room, and there was the baby, sound asleep. She was being Jane today. What time was it, anyway? How long had she been asleep? It felt like she had slept for a day or two. She quietly tiptoed down the steps to the kitchen and looked out the window at the ocean, the beautiful, beckoning ocean.

When had she eaten? She hadn't had anything since she came here, she didn't eat at the party or before the concert last night – was that last night? Why didn't she really feel hungry? She opened the refrigerator and didn't see anything that looked appetizing. She began looking through the upper cupboards and was amused to see the types of foods Jane and Sharla had, not like the exclusive food she chose to eat. They had sweet snacks, white bread, all kinds of chips and canned food. Hans would never allow this type of food in her kitchen. What would he fix for her on a day like today? He might start with a light, fluffy omelet, full of vegetables. She opened the refrigerator again. Yes, they had eggs, although they were not marked as being from grain-fed free-range hens. They had an onion and a green pepper, although they were not labeled as 'certified organic.' She didn't see any spinach or soy cheese or garlic pepper, and the cooking oil in the cupboard was not olive oil, but she decided she could put together something she could digest.

Where would they keep a frying pan? She looked through the lower cupboards and found other pots and pans, but no frying pan. They must fry things, mustn't they? She looked at the oven and noticed there seemed to be a drawer underneath it. Sure enough, it opened and it held a variety of frying pans and baking sheets. She selected a medium-size frying pan and began her new adventure – to cook for herself. She spent a few minutes figuring out how to make the stove work, then she whipped up two eggs in a bowl and poured them in a frying pan with hot oil. It immediately began to spatter, so she turned down the heat on the burner. She chopped the green peppers and onion, and by the time she was ready to add them, the egg was already cooked. She poured them into the pan anyway, folded the egg over them, turned off the burner and scooped the concoction onto a plate. She did it! She could cook for herself!

Leeza poured a glass of orange juice – not fresh squeezed, and not organic, but orange juice just the same, and she sat at the table to eat. The egg was bland, but it tasted good. The orange juice tasted weird, but she figured that some people lived on this type of food, so she could, too, for one day. She finished eating and put her dishes in the sink. She then went to the closet to look at the red cloak – she had to be sure it was still there, so she could make her escape from this place in the evening. Yes, there was the cloak, hanging there in all its redness. She closed the closet door. This was a great life, for a day, but she couldn't stay here, in this life of obscurity, doing everything for herself, forever. She would love to call Gretchen to come over and give her a massage, but she knew she had to wait until she went home. She couldn't reveal her hiding place, her secret identity.

She wondered how Jane was doing at her house. She would be having it so easy, with everything and everyone at her beck and call. She'd be living it up, enjoying the good life, swimming in her own pool, having a massage or going in the hot tub, eating only the choicest foods, selected especially for her, and not having to clean up after herself. A scary thought popped into her mind... what if Jane didn't want to switch back? What if Jane decided to enjoy Leeza's life, and not come back to her own reality? Oh, no, Jane would not stay away from her baby forever. Obviously, Jane would like living Leeza's life for a short visit, but she would want to return to her life full of meaning, the life Leeza was beginning to understand and enjoy.

A cry broke into her thoughts. The baby was awake! Leeza charged up the steps and into Shari's room. Shari was lying in her crib, crying.

"What's the matter?" Leeza asked.

Shari continued to cry.

"Do you need another diaper change?" She picked up the baby and smelled her little pants. She didn't smell bad. Leeza pulled out the front of the pants and looked at the diaper – it seemed to be dry. Shari kept crying.

"What? Why are you crying? Aren't you happy?"

Leeza carried Shari downstairs and tried to comfort her. Shari calmed down a little then she began crying again. What did it mean? What did she want? Why didn't she just say it? Leeza set Shari in the playpen and she cried more loudly.

The front door opened and Sharla came in the house.

"What's the matter with Shari?" She rushed to the playpen.

"I don't know, I was hoping you would know," Leeza said. "She was asleep and she just woke up a few minutes ago, and she started crying."

"Did you change her?"

"Of course," Leeza said, pleased that she had done that by herself, at least.

"Did you give her a bottle?"

"Bottle?" Leeza hadn't thought of that. What would she put in a bottle, anyway? Milk?

"Jane, you idiot," Sharla said. "Where is your brain? You know she always has a bottle at this time."

"I forgot," Leeza said.

"Yeah, right, you are just so wrapped up in yourself! You are the most self-centered person I know!" Sharla rolled her eyes.

"I am not!"

"You probably didn't even notice the time, did you?"

"The time?"

"I knew I shouldn't have left Shari here alone with you."

"Why not?"

"Come on, get it together! You always do that, just to get out of being responsible. You are the most immature person in the world!"

"I am not!" Leeza replied. She didn't have any better defense.

"Mom's not doing well," Sharla said, as she prepared a bottle for Shari. Leeza discreetly watched to see how she did it: she took something out of a can and mixed it with water in a measuring cup, then poured the mixture into a bottle, shook it, and put it in the microwave oven. Leeza paid close attention to the way she turned on the microwave; she had never used one, but she decided it could be very handy when she wasn't in the same house with Hans. Hans would never allow a microwave in his kitchen, but this was a completely different type of kitchen, a completely different kind of life. She could almost see rays of radiation extending in all directions from the microwave, but, she reminded herself, many people lived by eating food cooked in a microwave oven. Sharla and Jane seemed to be fine, or at least they were living, and apparently they used a microwave often.

"Did you hear what I said?" Sharla asked, shaking the bottle, then squirting a few drops on her arm. She gave the bottle to Shari, who eagerly grabbed it and began drinking.

"Yeah, sure, I heard you," Leeza answered. She couldn't remember what she had said – she was focused on how Sharla had prepared the baby's bottle. How was she expected to respond?

"She didn't say anything," Sharla said, obviously disappointed.

"She didn't?" Leeza asked, wondering what she was talking about. Who didn't say anything about what? Was she expecting Shari to say something?

"Not one word," Sharla said, staring into the playpen.

"That's too bad," Leeza replied: a safe reply. She felt like Sharla was expecting her to say something else, but she had no idea what was the topic of conversation, so she also stared into the playpen, at Shari. Shari was thoroughly enjoying her bottle, holding it with her hands and her feet. Leeza smiled. She was in love with this baby!

"You should go see her," Sharla said. When Leeza didn't respond, she continued, "I know how you feel and everything, but you need to put that behind you and go see her."

Leeza was afraid to ask what she meant. If she said the wrong thing, Sharla would know she wasn't Jane, and the success of this whole charade depended on Leeza being Jane. She didn't say a word. She just kept watching Shari.

"You know, I don't even know if she would know who you are," Sharla confessed. "I doubt that she knew who I was today. She knew me yesterday. Come on, Jane, you haven't talked to her in so long. She's slipping away from us and this could be your last chance."

Leeza figured it out – Sharla was talking about their mother! She put the pieces together... Sharla went to visit her today, she wasn't doing well, she was having some type of memory problems, and Jane hadn't spoken to her in a long time. Well, that wasn't right. Leeza hadn't had a mother in years. Jane should not neglect her own mother; she had been taking it for granted that she had a mother, that she would always be there, just waiting for her to come back to her whenever she got ready. Didn't she realize that she could be gone at any time, just like that, without ever another chance to make peace with her?

CHAPTER 7

"You're right," Leeza said softly.

"What?" Sharla said, startled.

"You are right. I should go see her."

"Jane! I can't believe it! That's the most wonderful thing you've said to me in a long, long time!"

"I don't want to miss my chance," Leeza explained. Maybe she could say to Jane's mother all the things she never had a chance to say to her own mother, before she lost her. Maybe she could step into Jane's place and do something good for both her and her mother. Her heart felt warmed, thinking of doing something to help someone besides herself.

"You know, last week when she was feeling better, I wasn't going to tell you this, but, remember when I hugged you when I came home, and you asked me what that was for?"

"Yes..." Leeza said tentatively.

"Well, that hug was from her," Sharla said. "She told me to give you a hug from her, but not tell you it was from her."

A tear formed in the corner of Leeza's eye. That was one of the saddest things she had ever heard. She couldn't imagine a mother and daughter with such a gap between them that the mother would have to give her daughter a hug through someone else – and then not even tell her it was a hug from her.

"So... when do you think you're gonna go?"

"This afternoon." Leeza stated. It had to be today.

"Wow, really? After all this time, you're ready now?"

"There's no time like the present," Leeza said, quoting one of her songs. That was one of her catch phrases, an excuse to do what she wanted to do when she wanted to do it.

"What made you change your mind, all of a sudden? All this time, you wanted nothing to do with her, and now, suddenly, you're going to go see her?"

"Watching Shari makes me realize how fragile life is," Leeza explained.

"Wow, you are really growing up in a hurry," Sharla said.

"You have to come with me," Leeza insisted. She had no idea where to go!

"Yeah, Mom might freak out if you just showed up. She probably wouldn't know who you are."

"Of course she will! A mother never forgets her children!"

"You haven't seen her in such a long time."

"She'll know me! She has to! She has to know her own daughter!"

"No, I mean, you don't know what she's like now. Her memory is just about gone, and I don't mean, like she used to be forgetful. It's like, she usually doesn't even know who she is."

Leeza began to get the picture. Now she knew she had to see their mother. She had to reconcile, not only for Jane and her mother, but for herself as well. She had so many things she needed to tell her own mother, who had been gone for too many years, who had left her without giving her any final instructions, without giving her a chance to say goodbye.

"We'll have to go tomorrow morning. I can't go this afternoon," Sharla said. "Some of us have to work, you know."

"Work?" Leeza asked.

"Yeah, I know, it's a foreign word to you, but someone around here has to pay the bills."

Leeza smiled, thinking of what a small amount they must pay for this house, what a small amount Sharla would have to earn to pay the bills around here. One of Leeza's shows would pay for the house, as well as all the bills, for the next ten years.

She wondered where Sharla worked, but she couldn't ask. Sharla would expect her, as Jane, to know these kinds of things.

"Okay, tomorrow morning we'll go," Leeza agreed. She would need to convince Jane to stay in her life for one more day. She was sure Jane was just living it up, having fun, eating gourmet food, and being Leeza.

"Hmmm, I wish we could go today, before you change your mind," Sharla said thoughtfully.

"Me too!" Leeza said.

"But we can't," Sharla said, shaking her head.

"I'm not going to change my mind."

"Yeah, you say that now, but I know you."

"I'm not going to change my mind!"

"You're so sure now, but tomorrow you... ah, never mind. I just hope you still want to go tomorrow. I have to get ready for work."

"What? What?" Leeza asked, wanting to know more about Jane. Why would her sister be talking about her like that?

"I'm just glad you want to go see Mom, and I hope you are still in this frame of mind tomorrow."

"Tomorrow, I will be," Leeza said. The next day, she couldn't predict, since Jane would be back then, but tomorrow, she was sure. She had to speak to their mother. If she hadn't seen Jane in such a long time, she wouldn't know she wasn't Jane. Leeza had fooled Jane's own sister; why couldn't she fool their mother? Leeza's forte was performing, and this was an opportunity to give the most magnificent performance of her life (up to this point).

As Sharla went upstairs to get ready for work, Shari cooed, grabbing Leeza's attention. What a meaningful life Jane had! All she had to do was live on the beach, take care of her baby, get to know her baby, and hang around in this nice, homey home. Yes, that's what it was, homey. The whole house invited her to just sit back and live there, and enjoy life. The scent of the wood mixed with the ocean, the earthy colors and the decorations, all so carefully placed right where they belonged. The house was so familiar, it made Leeza feel as if this were her own home.

Leeza picked up Shari and held her close to her body. Shari smelled so good, like babies usually do, and she was so warm, so trusting. This baby relied on Jane for everything, for her very life. Jane had such a sweet life, an important life, a life that this small person depended on for her own life. Leeza was really adapting to playing the role of being Jane.

"Come on, Shari," Sharla said.

"Where's she going?" Leeza asked.

"To the baby sitter, of course," Sharla said. "Are you going to be okay by yourself?"

"Why is she going to a baby sitter?" Leeza asked, not wanting to let her go. "She can stay here with me."

"We are not having this discussion," Sharla said. "Here, give her to me."

Leeza reluctantly gave Shari to Sharla, with her mind full of questions about the situation. Why would Sharla be taking Jane's baby to a baby sitter when Jane stayed home all day long? What was the matter with Jane? She couldn't ask any of the questions, or she would make Jane seem worse than she apparently was.

CHAPTER 8

Leeza watched Sharla and Shari leave, then she darted upstairs to Jane's room. Maybe she kept a diary or something, some kind of clue to her life. She wasn't really a Plain Jane, after all; she was a Complicated Jane. Leeza frantically searched her dresser, her desk, but she didn't find a diary. She stopped searching and began to look at the room, really look at it. Besides being a huge mess, it was very comfortable. The furniture was beautiful, as if it had been chosen specifically for this room. The window had a window seat, and with the exception of all the red in the room, this bedroom was as if Leeza herself had decorated it.

Where in this room would she put any personal information? To put it in the desk would be too obvious. No, she wouldn't even hide anything under her clothes in a drawer. She would have a secret place... like inside the window seat! She moved the pillows and tried to lift the seat. She pulled each side, looked for hinges, then she decided that it didn't open. She went over to the desk and sat in the chair. She hadn't found a diary, but she should be able to find something else with a part of Jane's personality in it. In the center drawer were pens, pencils, gum and stacks of stickie notes – all blank. She opened one of the side drawers and found a small photo album and a stack of magazines. As she picked up the photo album, she noticed her own face on the cover of the top magazine. Her face was on the next one and the next one and the next one – Jane was a fan of hers! Every magazine in the drawer had Leeza's face on the cover! Jane even had some Leeza herself hadn't seen. She opened the photo album and began looking through the photos. There were several pictures of Sharla and Jane, a few of Sharla and Shari, one with Jane holding Shari, and one – only one – with Sharla and Jane and their mother, a long time ago. They must have been in their early teens at that time. Then, near the end of the book, were several photos of Leeza on stage, several years ago. Leeza looked so much younger in these photos. She tried to remember when and where these photos were taken – the stage didn't look familiar – but she had done so many shows in so many places, she couldn't be expected to remember every one, could she? She certainly didn't remember this one.

She turned back to the photo of the girls with their mother. Jane looked like Leeza even then, a young, innocent version of Leeza. Their mother had a distant look, as if she were a million miles away.

Where was this one taken? The background revealed no indication of any particular place, but the photo seemed so familiar, like she had seen this one before, a long, long time ago, before she became famous.

Were these all the photos Jane had? That seemed rather strange. Leeza moved to the bookcase. Jane must be quite a reader, with all these books. Leeza hadn't heard of any of these titles. Some of them were textbooks – how boring. Maybe Jane was one of those perpetual students, taking classes and studying all the time, but never finishing school. Leeza wondered about that – but only for a moment. She had to find some hints, some kind of information about Jane's life! Where would it be, if not in her bedroom?

Leeza spotted a book titled "Securing Your Future." What would that hold for Jane? As Leeza opened it, she noticed dollars between the pages – no, not dollars, but hundred dollar bills. There must have been at least 40 or 50 in there. Why would Jane have all this money hidden in a book? Where had she gotten it?

Leeza looked around the room again, then she began to feel antsy. Yes, by now she would have finished her workout with her personal trainer. She needed some exercise. She could go for a run on the beach! Running barefoot on sand was so comforting. She found some shorts in Jane's drawer – it was a good thing they were both the same size – and she got dressed to go running.

Leeza ran and ran and ran, she didn't know how long, then she turned around and ran all the way back to the beach area in front of Jane's house. She felt so good! Her legs felt strengthened, her lips tasted salty, and her toes were loving the warm sand. She ran into the water, just a short distance, to cool her feet and legs, and then she went back to the steps leading up to the house. She sat on the top step and looked at the ocean, the massive, moving, beautiful ocean, waving and waving at her. She could get comfortable in this simple life. What if she didn't have to constantly deal with all the people in her household, the people on her staff? What if dozens of people didn't depend on her to support them? What if she could just sit here, like this, every day, in anonymity, and enjoy nature? That type of life would be so relaxing!

But, no, she couldn't live like that. She craved excitement, adoration, lots of people always paying attention to her and taking care of her every need. She was famous for setting trends and her endorsements made unknown artists and nameless items popular. She had been famous for more than a few years, and she could probably ride this tide for at least another ten or twenty years, which would then provide a nice retirement for her. She could look forward to that time, when she could sit like this in a place like this. She would have to consult with Jack-Boy and get him to purchase a nice little house on the beach for her, maybe even one in this general area.

She thought about her rise to stardom, and how she had been chosen out of millions for that path. Yes, she knew she had the look that sold magazines, the look that every teenage girl wanted, with the long, silky, shiny hair, the large, blue, doe eyes, the peaches and cream smooth complexion, the long, slender legs, the small waist and the nice, firm breasts; but her voice wasn't outstanding, nor were her dance moves unique. However, once she was selected to be the teen idol, she put everything she had into living up to the image. She practiced her dance moves until she could do them in her sleep. She took voice lessons and constantly sang her songs so she knew them forwards and backwards. She paid attention to her many coaches; she was mindful to not step out of line and she carefully controlled every aspect of her life. She followed all the rules and didn't take risks, so now, nearly ten years later, she was still on top, still in demand, still loved by her fans: she was still in control. Her life was so good.

As Leeza stared at the ocean, she couldn't remember a day when she had so much time to herself. Sure, she could be alone whenever she wanted, but she could constantly feel them milling outside her door, and waiting downstairs, to get something for her, to make something for her, to do something with her. That was not a good way to relax; that was more like just passing time until it was time for the next thing to happen. Jane should be basking in it, just for a day... oh, yeah, tonight she would have to tell Jane that she needed one more day here. She had no doubt that Jane would go along with the modified plan.

CHAPTER 9

Leeza stood up and stretched, inhaling the fresh, clean, ocean air. When would Sharla be home, she wondered. She already was missing Shari – she couldn't even imagine how much Jane must miss her. She quickly put that thought out of her mind while she went back inside the house. What did Jane do all day, anyway? She obviously didn't spend much time cleaning her room. She had all those books – maybe she did a lot of reading, or maybe she was taking some classes. Perhaps Jane liked to watch television – Leeza didn't have much use for it herself – she was the star of television programs, not a mere watcher – but she knew lots of people did waste a lot of time watching programs besides the ones in which she was a star.

This day was getting to be long and boring for Leeza. She didn't have anything to do, she didn't have anyone to keep her company. When would Sharla be home? Should she make something for dinner? What could she possibly make, given the limited selection in their kitchen? What was expected of her, of Jane, at this time of day?

Leeza returned to Jane's room. At least at her own house, Leeza had someone to take care of her clothes. Leeza always left her room looking like this, in complete disarray, but then when she came back to it, everything would be in its proper place. If Jane didn't put away her own clothes, should she expect Leeza to clean up after her? Leeza couldn't bring herself to do such a menial task. She shoved the clothes off the bed and pulled up the covers – not in any way to resemble making the bed, but just enough so she could lie across the bed and take a little nap. Her mind was racing, but her body was tired. She had had a busy weekend, and a busy day today. As she drifted to sleep, she kept in mind that she needed to awaken in time to meet Jane tonight. She could see all the things she needed to do in her real life, but that was a world away from her right now. All those things would just have to wait for her to come home.

Sounds of voices brought Leeza back to Jane's room. The room was darker, but not too dark to be able to see. She recognized Sharla's voice and then she heard her baby, Shari, making noises, calling to her mother. Leeza quickly rushed down the steps to the kitchen, where Sharla was fixing a snack for herself and for Shari.

"You hungry?" Sharla asked, without turning away from her concoction in the blender.

"Yeah, a little," Leeza answered, sitting at the table near Shari. She attempted to play with her, but she didn't really know what to do.

"Whoa! What happened to you?" Sharla shrieked, as she turned towards Leeza and Shari, pouring a mixture into a glass.

"What? What's wrong?" Leeza asked.

"Who are you?" Sharla asked. "I don't know you."

"What are you talking about?"

"You look like a completely different person."

"What do you mean?" Leeza made a face at Shari. Shari smiled at her.

"I mean, you don't look at all like yourself."

"I just took a nap, that's all."

"Yeah, right, sure," Sharla said. "I don't know who you are."

"I'm your sister!"

"Yeah, right. You expect me to believe that?"

"I'm the same person who told you this afternoon that I want to go see Mom."

"Are you sure?" Sharla tasted the drink, and then poured some into Shari's bottle. She returned to the blender.

"Sure, I'm sure! How would I know I said it if I didn't say it?"

"No, I mean, are you sure you still want to go see her? You haven't changed your mind?"

"No! I mean, yes! No, I haven't changed my mind, and, yes, I want to go see her!" She alternated nodding and shaking her head.

"Well, okay, I guess you're you," Sharla said.

"Who else would I be?" Leeza raised an eyebrow.

"You tell me."

Was this some kind of a trick? Sharla must realize that Leeza was not really her sister.

"I'm Jane, plain Jane."

"Come on, don't start feeling sorry for yourself."

"No, I'm glad to be who I am. So, what are you fixing?" She had to say anything to change the drift of this conversation!

"A strawberry mango smoothie. Want some?"

That almost sounded like something Hans would make for her.

"Sure! Sounds great!" She was getting really hungry by now.

"I didn't think you would want any. I thought you were on your chocolate kick."

"No, that's over," Leeza assured her. She loved chocolate, but she couldn't eat it. Chocolate, and the things that were mixed with it, did unkind things to her skin and to her digestion. She had to have lots of fruit every day, and a strawberry-mango smoothie was just what she needed right at this moment. "Do we have any yogurt?"

"Yogurt? Since when did you start liking yogurt?" Sharla asked suspiciously.

"It's an acquired taste, and I just acquired it," Leeza explained.

"No, we don't have any yogurt," Sharla said, "but I did bring some chicken from KFC. I got a variety pack."

The word 'chicken' made Leeza's stomach growl. She could smell it and it smelled fabulous! Sharla removed some items from a large red and white bag, and she began opening Styrofoam containers and cardboard boxes. Oh, no, the chicken was deep-fried... Leeza couldn't eat that. She only ate boneless, skinless, broiled chicken breasts. The potatoes looked like they were reconstituted and the corn on the cob was overcooked. The biscuits were made from white flour, and even the honey was not real. She couldn't eat any of this type of food... but Jane could. She had to eat this food to convince Sharla that she was really Jane.

She sat at the table, ready to be served. Sharla gave her a look of discontent and then handed her a paper plate and a plastic spoon-fork. Leeza tried to not cringe at the thought of eating from disposable ware, while at the same time concentrating on how Jane would be acting. She served herself small amounts of everything and waited for Sharla to begin eating. At her house, she was always served first, but no one ate until everyone was served – and they all waited for her to take the first bite. This seemed to be Sharla's domain; she was the one to follow. To Leeza's surprise, Sharla bowed her head in prayer. Leeza quickly dropped her head as Sharla blessed the food they were about to eat.

When the prayer ended, Leeza took a tiny taste of the crispy part of chicken. Oh, that tasted so good, it must have been sinful. She knew why this type of food was forbidden in Hans' kitchen... it was not real food! Hans didn't serve anything that did not have nutritional value. What was this stuff, anyway? Some great-tasting, fried blob of... what? It had a good crunch to it. She bit into the chicken, and although it was full of grease, it was delicious. Oh, she would have to apologize to her digestive system later, for putting this yummy-awful food into it. She finished the chicken quickly, and then downed the corn, the mashed potatoes and gravy, and the biscuit with the phony honey. The food sat in her stomach like a glob of clay, so she moistened it with her smoothie. Now, that was a nice smoothie, full and tasty.

"Wow, haven't you ever eaten before?" Sharla asked. Leeza became aware that Sharla was staring at her.

"I guess I was more hungry than I thought," Leeza said. "Thanks, Sis, that was really good. You did an excellent job on the smoothie."

"Yeah, no problem, *Sis*. Since when did you start calling me 'Sis,' anyway?"

"It just seemed appropriate now," Leeza said, as inconspicuously as possible.

"You are not my sister," Sharla said.

Leeza froze.

"I am," she said, holding her breath.

"You have never in your life thanked me for anything. Who is in your body, anyway? Or is this another Oprah experiment?"

"I had a reason to thank you tonight," Leeza said, as if that explained it.

"You are like a different person every day," Sharla began, and then she stopped. "I need to put Shari to bed." She got up from the table and removed Shari from her high chair.

"I can put her to bed," Leeza said. After all, she was supposed to be her mother.

"You just take it easy and put the dishes in the dishwasher, if it's not too much trouble," Sharla said, taking Shari upstairs.

Leeza looked at the food on the table and desired to eat more – but she couldn't let herself have another bite. Her diet was under strict control at all times, and she had already eaten too many items that were not on her personal menu. She put the tops on the containers and placed them in the refrigerator, and then she picked up the dishes, smiling to herself as she realized that Sharla had made a joke when she told her to put the dishes in the dishwasher. Leeza dropped them in the garbage can, and then she wiped the table with the sponge, satisfied with her execution of manual labor.

She slipped quickly up the steps so she could kiss Shari goodnight. Wasn't that what a mother should be doing? Sharla was just leaving Shari's room and she gave Leeza a questioning look.

"I just want to give her a goodnight kiss," she explained.

"Do whatever you want," Sharla said, then she added, "you always do. But don't get her all excited – she needs to go to sleep."

Leeza stepped into the baby's room, inhaling the baby scents, and she looked into the crib. Shari was already asleep, with just a kiss from her aunt, and not yet one from her mother. Leeza couldn't reach Shari's puffy cheek with her lips, so she kissed her own fingertips and then touched them gently to Shari's sweet baby skin.

"Goodnight, Mommy's angel," she said, repeating the phrase her mother had often said to her, so many lifetimes ago. Jane really had something special in her life, with this baby.

Leeza wanted to talk to Sharla, but she had closed her bedroom door, so Leeza went into Jane's room. What did Jane do all the time? She didn't have a computer or a TV in her room, she didn't have a job – or did she? All she had was a bookshelf full of books, dusty books that looked like they had been sitting on the shelves for ages.

Leeza checked the clock. She still had nearly four hours before she had to meet Jane. She didn't really want to take another nap, but what else was there to do in this life? She didn't have any kinds of games or hobbies in the room, and Leeza had a feeling that most of the items in the house were Sharla's, not Jane's. She could hear muffled sounds of a TV coming from Sharla's room. Maybe Sharla had taken in Jane and her baby. Yes, that was a logical explanation, since this room didn't really seem like it was home to Jane. It was more like a guest room, a room where Jane was staying temporarily. The books probably weren't even hers. Jane probably didn't know Sharla had all that money hidden in the book.

Leeza got the photo album again and turned to the picture of the girls with their mother. The setting was so familiar; the scene was like it came right out of some old movie. Leeza tried to imagine what they were doing that day, where they had been, who had taken the photo. Had it been their father? Where was he, anyway? She didn't see any signs of him anywhere in the house. He had probably left the family a long time ago, when the girls were still young.

Sharla and Jane had looked a lot more alike when they were young than they did now. Now Sharla's hair had darkened, and Jane's hair was so much longer than her sister's. It was amazing how much Jane and Leeza looked alike – more than these two sisters – enough alike that the other sister didn't even know Jane had been replaced.

Leeza thought about how much fun Jane would be having right now, fooling everyone at her house. They would just think Leeza was acting eccentric, playing a role, having fun doing something different in between her shows. Jane could do or say anything in Leeza's life, and nobody would suspect that it wasn't really Leeza. Even if she told them her name was Jane, they would play along with her, assuming she had just picked up a personality to perform, regardless of the details she explained. Oh, yes, Jane must be having a blast in her life! Leeza wouldn't be surprised if she wanted to stay there all week. Of course, they would have to switch places before her next show. No matter how big a fan of Leeza's Jane might be, she would never be able to sing and dance like Leeza.

Leeza began rehearsing her songs in her head, adding her dance moves. She needed to practice every day, to stay perfect. She had enough space in Jane's bedroom to do most of her moves, if she scaled them down a little, or a lot, in some cases. She watched herself in the reflection of the window, amazed at how good she was. She often impressed herself. It was no wonder she was loved by millions of fans, all over the world.

She worked up a sweat and went to the kitchen to get some water. She was slightly disappointed that they only had tap water, no bottled water, and they didn't even have a water filter – but she just needed a drink of water. She filled a glass and drank it, not liking the chlorine taste, checking the clock again. She still had nearly two hours before Jane would be out on the beach, but she wanted to go out now. The evening was lovely, and she opened the kitchen door – then she remembered the red cloak. She retrieved it from the closet and took it with her down to the beach.

CHAPTER 10

The ocean was roaring, as it always did, and the moon was full and bright, reflecting off the water and the sand. Leeza couldn't see anyone else on the beach. She realized that the house was in a rather secluded locale; only a few houses were on this beach. She walked north for a while, and then she stopped and put on the red cloak. Now she was hidden, now she was strange. Now no one could identify her on this beach – she was a stranger, and Jane was Jane. Leeza had never been in this place.

She turned and began to walk south, right along the water's edge. The atmosphere was excellent, not too cool, not too breezy. All she needed was Chad by her side. She really missed him when he went to New York, which, unfortunately, he did often, to advance his career as a model. He was so handsome. She recalled when they first met, when they were put together to do a video shoot. She had been instantly attracted to him, much to Jack-Boy's disappointment, and Chad had shown an immediate interest in her. Suddenly they were pictured together everywhere, and they were the couple of the year. They were ideal together – when they were together. He had asked her to come to New York for this week, but she had refused. She didn't really like New York when she wasn't working. She didn't want to spend all day hanging out in his apartment, while he was doing his photo shoots, which could last 16 hours a day. He wouldn't have any time for her there. She preferred to wait for him to come back to the West Coast for their next rendezvous. She was really glad she had stayed here so she would have this opportunity to live Jane's life for a couple of days. She was a firm believer that everything happened for a reason.

Leeza wondered what time it was. It must be nearly one o'clock by now. She scanned the horizon, trying to see anyone walking on the beach. Jane should be getting close to the meeting place. Leeza quickened her pace. Although it was dark, the moon gave enough light so she could see that she was the only person in this area. She wasn't yet at the appointed place, but she could tell that Jane wasn't there yet either. Leeza wasn't worried – it could still be too early, or Jane could be running late.

Leeza circled their meeting spot, once, twice, three times. She would stay here until Jane arrived, walking, watching, waiting. She had to convince Jane that she needed just one more day here, in her life. Meeting Jane's mother was of utmost importance to Leeza, for many personal reasons of her own. Leeza could not allow Jane to say no to this request; Leeza needed to speak to her mother.

She decided not to tell Jane why she required the extra day here. Since Jane had not seen her mother in years, she might not be happy to learn that Leeza was going to visit her in her stead. Leeza really wanted to discover what had happened between Jane and her mother, what was the problem that had driven a wedge between them, but she couldn't just ask Jane about it. Jane would become suspicious if Leeza made any mention of her mother or their relationship. Jane had access to everything about Leeza's life; every aspect of her life was an open book, put on public display, so Jane could find out anything about Leeza that she didn't already know...but how could Leeza learn more about Jane's life?

Leeza paced around the meeting spot. Where was Jane? Surely it was well past two o'clock by now. Why didn't Leeza wear a watch? Oh, yes, other people always told her when it was time to do everything; she didn't need to keep track of time. She had left her iPod and her cell phone in the limo, thinking she wouldn't need them – now she needed them just for their clocks! She had no choice but to continue to wait for Jane to arrive. She couldn't go back to the house – what if Jane decided to just go home? Dennis or some fan could easily follow her, and then their cover would be blown, their secret identity switch would be revealed. No, Leeza had to stay here until Jane came, even if it meant waiting all night.

CHAPTER 11

After what seemed like another hour, Leeza sensed – she didn't hear or see - another person on the beach. She looked into the darkness, which was getting darker as the moon was moving out over the ocean, straining her eyes to see someone. Yes, a person was approaching; no, two people were approaching. She quickly slithered over to a huge driftwood log on the beach, hoping they hadn't noticed her. She relaxed a little – even if they had seen her, all they could have seen was a cloaked person. They had no way of knowing she was Leeza Hamilton, the famous performer.

While hidden behind the huge log, she watched the couple cavort, tango, slow dance, hug – and then kiss, kiss, kiss. They were obviously in love with each other, touching, feeling, holding each other. Leeza felt uneasy watching them from her hiding place, but they had to realize they were in a public place and anybody could be watching them. Leeza herself had experienced that with Chad. She had just wanted him to hold her and kiss her, aware that they had an audience everywhere they went, and she didn't care. She loved Chad, and it didn't matter to her what anyone else saw when she was with him.

The couple slowly moved away from each other, touching fingertips as they parted, becoming two people instead of one couple. As one person headed in the opposite direction, the other person started walking straight towards the log where Leeza was hiding. She considered running, then she decided to stay where she was. She wouldn't be able to run while wearing this cloak. Maybe this person hadn't seen her and didn't know she was there.

As the person approached, she recognized herself: it was Jane, with her hair styled just like Leeza often had hers styled. Jane knew she was there. Who was that guy that had been with her? It couldn't have been Chad. Well, one midnight date wouldn't damage Leeza's reputation. She had had lots of prop dates, arranged to keep her in the spotlight. Jane's little indiscretion could be good for Leeza's publicity, just to stir up interest in her, especially if one of those tabloid photographers had captured them on film.

"Hi, Jane," Leeza said, as she stepped out from behind the log.

"I knew you were there," Jane said.

"I wasn't hiding," Leeza said. "I just thought you might want a little privacy. Beautiful evening for romance."

"It's always beautiful here. So, how did everything go?" Jane asked. "Did Sharla get suspicious? She must have noticed you weren't me."

"She just seems to be suspicious," Leeza said. "Really, I think Shari knew I wasn't you."

"Oh, yeah, she would know, for sure," Jane agreed, nodding.

"But she didn't tell."

"Good for her!"

"Did anyone at my house...?" Leeza began.

"Everybody just thinks you are weird and manipulative and selfish."

"Thanks," Leeza said, crossing her arms.

"I'm just telling the truth, I mean, this is what they are saying."

"They told you that?"

"They think you never listen to them, so they just say what they want to say. They had no idea I was listening."

"Wow, really? I didn't know that." Leeza was always wrapped up in her own business, and she never really paid attention to what the household staff was saying. Their conversation didn't involve her. She didn't have time to try to figure out their problems. After all, she was paying them to take care of her problems.

"Well, thanks for the massage and everything. It was really nice, for one day. I wouldn't want to live your life forever. Too many people asking too many questions, and you don't have any time to yourself, or any space of your own. Give me the cloak." Jane reached out her hand, beckoning.

"I need to stay here, just for one more day," Leeza insisted.

"No way." Jane shook her head.

"Come on! Just one more day!"

"No! I want my own life back!" Jane stomped her foot on the sand.

"You'll get it! Tonight! I just need one more day here!"

"What for?"

"There's something I need to do."

"What can you possibly do here that you can't do in your own life? You can do whatever you want, whenever you want."

"I can't explain it. I just need another day."

"No! I want to go home!" Jane kept her hand extended, waiting for the cloak.

"Just go back to my house for one more day, and late tonight we'll switch back," Leeza pleaded.

"I am so tired! Every moment of my day was filled with people asking what I wanted to eat, what I wanted to do, where I wanted to go, did I want to take this phone call or see that person! Every minute! The only time I could relax was while I was getting a massage!"

Leeza nodded. She could use a massage right now. "You can just close the door to your room and tell everyone you don't want to be bothered, or you have a headache, or you want to take a nap or something. Or you can go swimming or get in the hot tub, or have Dennis take you for a drive. You can do whatever you want!" She wished there were enough light so Jane could see the convincing look on her face.

"If your life is so great, why don't you want to go back?"

"I do want to go back, but just not right now."

"Why?"

"I just need to do something with your sister tomorrow – or, later today, I mean," Leeza confessed.

"Like what?"

"We just need to finish a conversation. If you go home and she starts asking you about it, then you won't know what to say, and she will really know something is up."

"So what? She thinks I'm crazy anyway. I need to go home to my baby."

"Your baby is fine! We had a great day! Come on, I just need one more day to finish what I started."

"You weren't supposed to start anything!" Jane shouted.

"I know, but I did. I couldn't help it. I'll take care of it, and then you can come back tonight."

"Why don't we both go to my house and just tell Sharla the truth?" Jane grabbed Leeza's arm to pull her in the direction of the house.

"No!" Leeza yanked her arm away. "One of us needs to go back with Dennis, so my staff won't get suspicious."

"Oh, really, are you telling me you've never stayed away all night?"

"Not without letting someone know where I was. I have a lot of people depending on me."

"Yeah, right."

"All the people you met today, I pay their salaries!"

"Yeah, you are so important. That's why you need to go home to your house and you need to let me go home to my house."

"Tonight! Meet me here tonight! Come on! Just one more day! Enjoy yourself! It's a free vacation, with everything you could possibly want!"

"But not my baby, and not my life."

"Just one more day, I promise. Let me finish what I started, and then we'll go home, both of us, to our own homes tonight."

"What is so important that you have to stay? And why won't you tell me?"

"I'll tell you tonight, I promise."

"Forget it."

"Jane! Okay, I'll pay you. How much?"

"I said, forget it. I'm going home, with or without the cloak."

"Wait!" Leeza shouted. She paused and composed herself. "Just do this, one more day, just for me? It's really important to me. I'll explain everything tomorrow night."

"Just one more day."

"Just one more day."

"You promise."

"I promise."

"Let's just go home and discuss it."

"There's nothing to discuss!"

"Yes, there is!"

"No! Besides, we don't want to wake up the baby and your sister."

"Let's meet here at eleven o'clock, instead of one," Jane suggested.

"Sure, fine, that's great," Leeza agreed. "Indulge yourself all day. Do whatever you want. That's what everyone will be expecting me to do, so you do it, for yourself."

"Yeah, whatever."

"Hey, who was that guy?"

"Well, that's my secret and I'll tell you about him tonight," Jane said, "right after you tell me what your secret is."

"It's not a secret, it's just something I need to do. Now, get back to the limo before Dennis comes looking for me."

"You know, I really don't like you telling me what to do."

"Okay! I won't! Just go!" Leeza shooed Jane away from her.

"Tonight at eleven," Jane said.

"Tonight at eleven," Leeza promised.

"See you then."

CHAPTER 12

Leeza headed up the beach to the house while Jane made her way to the parking lot where Dennis was waiting for her with the limousine. Leeza had to get some sleep so she would be ready for her visit to Jane's mother in a few hours.

Once she crawled into Jane's bed, Leeza couldn't sleep. So many things were running through her mind. She rehearsed what she would say to Jane's mother at least fifty times, with every possible variation of how her mother might respond. Her body was excessively tired, but her mind was racing a mile a minute. She tried to relax by taking deep breaths, but that didn't work. She tried counting backwards from 100, but by the time she was down to 84, her mind had taken off in another direction. She was excited, anticipating the meeting. She was also afraid that she would lose her courage before she could say everything she wanted to say. She pictured their mother in her mind, the mother of long ago, when they were girls. She tried to imagine how her voice would have sounded back then, what kinds of phrases she would have used when she spoke to them, how she would have encouraged and comforted her daughters.

Leeza considered her plans. She was going to go to see Jane's mother, as Jane, and say all the things Leeza never had had a chance to tell her own mother, before she was gone. Leeza had left home without saying goodbye, then she had ridden to stardom without looking back at her family, without checking in with them, until the day she heard that her mother had died. She hadn't gone to the funeral – she was much too busy to take time out of her schedule that week – she had performances four nights in a row. She stayed busy, suppressing her feelings, not thinking about what she had missed: until this opportunity presented itself, an opportunity to tell Jane's mother, in place of her mother, all the things she needed to say. She would tell her she didn't blame her for driving her out of the house, that it had been all her own choice to leap for a chance to become a star and live the grand lifestyle. She would thank her for being supportive of her when she was younger, thank her for instilling in her the confidence she needed to pursue her dream. Most importantly, she would tell her she loved her. Then somehow, her own mother would get the message sent to her in heaven, and they could have peace between them. Leeza would finally be able to stop feeling guilty for leaving home, so long ago, without her mother's blessing.

The smell of bacon awakened Leeza. She had drifted to sleep in the wee hours of the morning, and now she was feeling completely refreshed. She quickly selected a cute outfit of Jane's – all her outfits were cute, but none were really stylish – and got dressed. She deliberately didn't put on any make-up, in order to appear more plain than Leeza usually looked. She admired herself in the mirror, assured that Jane's mother would be so happy to see her daughter looking like this. She skipped down the steps to the kitchen.

"Good morning!" she announced.

"You're bright and chipper this morning," Sharla said, standing over the stove in her bathrobe.

"What time are we going?" Leeza asked.

"Going? Where?" Sharla seemed puzzled.

"To see Mom!"

"You still want to go? I don't really feel like going today."

Leeza wanted to ask Sharla where their mother was so she could go by herself, but she couldn't let on that she didn't know.

"There's no time like the present!" she said, recalling she had told her that yesterday.

"Yeah, yeah, yeah," Sharla said, yawning, "but I'm so tired."

"Just go with me, and then you can leave, right after we get there," Leeza begged.

"I'm just too tired to get Shari ready and everything."

"I'll get her ready!" Leeza was bursting with energy – how hard could it be to get a baby ready to go somewhere? Shouldn't she be doing it, anyway? She was supposed to be Shari's mother. Sharla was really taking her aunt duties too far.

"Well, okay..." Sharla said tentatively, focusing on the bacon and eggs she was fixing.

"So what time are we going? Do you want me to get her ready now? Or do you have to do something else before we go?" Leeza was really getting excited.

"We're going to eat before we do anything," Sharla said, "and Shari needs to eat, too."

"Yeah, sure, of course," Leeza said.

"What has gotten into you?"

"I'm just really geared up."

"You haven't acted like this in years."

"I haven't felt this good in years!"

"Wow, we better go early, before you lose your enthusiasm."

"Yeah, whenever you're ready, I'm ready!"

"You really are ready."

"I really am!"

Sharla put the bacon and eggs on the table and grabbed a jar of baby food for Shari. As she began prepare her food, Leeza stopped her.

"I'll feed her," she offered. It seemed to be so fun yesterday when Sharla fed her.

"Yeah, okay, go ahead," Sharla said, handing the baby spoon and jar of food to Leeza. Shari watched them both with wide eyes.

"Come on, Sweetheart, open up," Leeza said, opening her mouth, as an example to Shari. Shari looked at her uncertainly, then she opened her mouth also and took the bite of food.

"Good girl! Now, say 'ahhhh,' come on," Leeza coaxed.

Shari opened her mouth again. This was easy! Feeding a baby was a fun and rewarding little job! Leeza was fully concentrating on getting the bites of food in the mouth, scraping up the overflow, and shoving it back into the mouth, that cute, little, delicate mouth. Before she knew it, the jar was empty and Shari was still waiting with an open mouth.

"That's all, Darling," she said.

"Give her a bottle if she's still hungry," Sharla said.

"Should she be eating so much?"

"She knows when to stop eating."

"I think she's finished, for now," Leeza observed.

"Yeah, that should be enough for now. I can give her a bottle when we get back home. I'm going to get ready to go. Put on her jogging outfit."

Shari had a jogging outfit? Leeza couldn't wait to see it. She cleaned up Shari's face and high chair and, after figuring out how to remove the tray, she lifted Shari and took her upstairs to her room. Sharla expected her to know where to find the jogging outfit, so she couldn't ask her where it was. She set Shari in the crib while she searched the little cabinets and tiny dresser. She found the cutest little light pink jogging suit that had a white stripe down the legs. Shari was going to look so fashionable in it!

Leeza removed Shari's nightgown and noticed she needed a clean diaper. She, the experienced diaper-changer, had the dirty one off and the clean one on her in no time, and then she put on the little jogging suit. Shari was such a doll! Leeza even found a tiny pair of

Nikes and some little sport socks that completed the look. Her baby was looking good! She picked her up and gave her a big hug. Mmmm, she smelled so good, Leeza had to kiss her forehead. Her baby hair was so soft, her skin was so fresh... babies were really fascinating creatures! She would miss Shari when she went back to her own life. Maybe Jane would let her come and visit on occasion.

Sharla shuffled into Shari's room dressed in baggy lounging clothes.

"You don't feel good, do you?" Leeza asked.

"Do I look that bad?"

"No, you don't look bad, you just look like you don't feel good."

"Let's just go and get this over with."

"Are you ready?" Leeza asked, raising an eyebrow.

"Would I be telling you to go if I weren't ready?"

"No, I mean, you got ready so fast."

Sharla went down the steps and Leeza followed, carrying Shari. She wondered if she should know something about their outing, like to put Shari in a stroller or bring a baby bag or put a blanket around her. She didn't say anything, waiting for a cue or a clue from Sharla.

Sharla didn't give her any type of hint, so Leeza assumed that she wasn't overlooking anything. Sharla went out the front door with Leeza and Shari right behind her. Sharla didn't lock the door, nor did she tell Leeza to lock the door, so she didn't lock it, she just closed it. Leeza wondered if they would be walking or going by car, so she just continued to follow Sharla's lead. She shifted Shari to the other shoulder – she was getting kind of heavy.

CHAPTER 13

They had walked about two blocks when Sharla turned onto a sidewalk to an older house. Was this their mother's house? What was the matter with her? Why had Sharla said she was 'slipping away' if she lived in a nice house like this? Leeza had assumed that their mother was in a hospital or a nursing home, or some kind of adult care facility, but she had been wrong in that assumption.

Sharla knocked on the door while Leeza stood tentatively behind her, holding Shari, trying to sneak a look at the surroundings that, presumably, were familiar to Jane. She thought it was kind of odd that Sharla was knocking on her own mother's door, but she wasn't in a position to question anything Sharla did.

A very kind-looking lady answered the door, not the lady from the photograph. Leeza didn't say anything. She would let Sharla do the talking, at least for now. Why didn't Sharla embrace her, or say something? Was this their mother?

Leeza followed them into the house, taking a good look at the interior. Nothing seemed familiar – the family photos had a large group of people that didn't include Jane and Sharla. They stopped in a room that Leeza would label as a sitting room, with old-fashioned Victorian couches and little cherry wood tables.

"How is she today?" Sharla asked, keeping her voice low.

This was not their mother, Leeza realized. This must be someone else, maybe another relative. Had Jane been here before? Leeza wasn't sure how she should act, so she bounced Shari on her hip as she searched the room for some kind of an indication as to whose house this was.

"She is not well," the lady said. "Are you both here to see her?" she asked uncertainly, throwing an uneasy look at Leeza.

"Yes," Sharla said, "but just for a minute. We don't want to tire her."

"Just for a minute," the lady agreed. She led them to a side room and slowly opened the door. "Ruby, you have company," she said softly.

Their mother's name was Ruby! That triggered a memory in Leeza's mind, but she couldn't quite grasp it. Who was Ruby? She peered over Sharla's shoulder so she might have a look at her. All she could see was the silhouette of a woman who was sitting in a wheelchair, looking out the window. She made no sound, no move to acknowledge their presence.

Sharla slowly approached their mother. She was about to put her hand on her shoulder when she suddenly withdrew it. She squatted beside the wheelchair.

"Mom?" she said quietly. "Mom, it's me, Sharla, Mom. Mom, can you hear me?"

Leeza felt a huge lump growing in her throat. She had had no idea it was going to be like this. She held Shari close to her, to stifle a cry that wanted to start.

"Mom," Sharla began again, "I brought someone with me." She motioned for Leeza to hand Shari to her. "Look, Mom, it's your granddaughter, Shari. Shari, say hi to Grandma."

Shari grabbed at her grandmother's hair, but she still didn't respond.

Leeza noticed that the other lady had left the room and shut the door. This was her chance, maybe her final chance, to speak and maybe mend a bridge between Jane and her mother. She had to speak now.

"Hi, Mom," she said boldly. "Mom, it's me. Hellooooo, Mom!"

Their mother seemed to snap out of a trance. She turned and looked at Sharla and Shari, then she turned around to see Leeza. Leeza smiled as their mother looked her over, from head to toe.

"Mom, we both wanted to come and see you today," Sharla began.

"You are not my daughter," their mother said to Leeza. She turned back to the window.

Leeza was stunned. How did she know she wasn't Jane? How could she tell? Sharla said Jane hadn't seen her in a long time.

"Mom! I AM your daughter!" Leeza insisted.

"Mom, come on, please forgive her. She came to make peace with you."

"I do not know this woman," Ruby said.

Leeza was shocked. First, she didn't like to be called a 'woman' – 'lady,' that was okay, 'girl' was fine; but 'woman'? She didn't know if Ruby really knew that Leeza wasn't her daughter, or if, as Sharla implied, Ruby had disowned Jane for some reason.

"Mom, I just want to talk to you," Leeza said, but it was too late. Ruby had slipped away from them, into her own world. Sharla kept urging her to talk, to come back to them, to look at her granddaughter, but she had no success. Ruby was gone.

"She's staying with me for a shorter and shorter time each day," Sharla said. "I'm really sorry she wouldn't talk to you. Sometimes she doesn't know me, either."

"Let's not talk about it here," Leeza said.

"Why not? She can't hear us."

"Yes, she can! Mom, I know you can hear us, on some level," Leeza said, holding back tears that wanted to flow. "Mom, I have some things to tell you. Mom! Don't ignore me!"

"She's not ignoring you! She can't hear you! That's what her disease does to her! That's what I've been telling you, all this time! You never pay attention to what I say!"

"Let me talk to her alone."

"I'm not leaving you alone with her." Sharla shook her head.

"I need to talk to her."

"We have to go."

"I just need a few minutes alone with her."

"Can't you see she's gone?"

"She's not gone!" Leeza looked at Ruby, wondering how to bring her back.

"You never can face reality, can you? You and your fantasy life! Welcome to the real world! Our mother's mind is gone! Can't you see it for yourself?"

"Her mind is not gone! She is just ignoring me!"

"You think it's all about you, don't you? This time, it's not about you! She is sick!"

"Don't say that, right behind her, in the same room with her! She can hear us, I know she can!"

"How would you know? You haven't been coming to see her! You don't know what she's like!"

"I'm here now, and I can see her! Mom, I can see you, and I know what you are doing! Mom, I just want to apologize to you!"

"It's kinda late for that, don't you think?"

"This is between me and Mom!"

"Yeah, that's it, you finally come to say you're sorry when she has no idea who you are! She isn't even aware that we are here!"

Shari began to cry.

"Now look what you've done!" Sharla said, trying to comfort the baby.

"You're the one who's been yelling!"

"Yeah, everything is always my fault! I'M the one who has been coming to see Mom every day! I'M the one who takes care of everything, while you do… NOTHING!"

Leeza didn't want to argue in the room with their mother. She wanted to just talk to her, face-to-face, but Sharla wouldn't let her.

"Let's just go," Sharla said, taking Shari towards the door.

"I want to stay a few minutes," Leeza said softly.

"I'm not leaving you alone with her."

"Then let's just stay a few more minutes," Leeza said. "Let's just sit quietly with her."

"What for? She doesn't even know we are here."

Leeza didn't answer, she just stayed rooted in place. She needed a few minutes with this woman, this mother, this familiar stranger. She walked over to her and gently stroked her hair. She could see bright red strands mixed in with the gray, ruby red strands. She closed her eyes and wished she could go back in time… an impossible desire.

"Baby," Ruby said softly. A tear ran down her cheek.

Leeza jumped. She saw was Sharla about to say something, and she put her finger to her lips to keep her quiet. Ruby was still staring out the window – but from this position, Leeza could see what she saw – the reflection of Sharla holding Shari.

"The constant arguing makes the baby cry," Ruby said.

"Mom?" Sharla said.

Ruby didn't answer.

"Mom?" Leeza said, very softly.

"You are not my daughter! Get away from me!" Ruby shrieked.

Leeza withdrew and hurried to the door. She yanked it open and ran out of the house.

CHAPTER 14

Coming to visit their mother had been a mistake. Leeza had had a selfish motive in mind, and it had turned out all wrong. She had thought her intentions were good. She had thought she could fix three lives at one time – hers, Jane's and Ruby's. Now she needed to get back to her own life, away from Jane's twisted world. She ran all the way to the house and flew up the steps to Jane's room. She slammed the door and collapsed onto the bed. She hated this stupid, Plain Jane life!

She let herself drown in her tears of selfishness. No one should have to put up with this kind of treatment – surely she, Leeza Hamilton, shouldn't! People served her, adored her, pampered her – they didn't ridicule her! Nobody told her to get away from them! Everybody wanted to be near her! They all wanted to live her life – they all wanted to BE her!

Leeza felt she must get away from here right now. She couldn't wait for Jane to meet her tonight. She would have to get her to come this morning. Leeza went down to the coat closet and pulled out the hideous red cloak, which was even more revolting in the light of day. She had to leave now, and she couldn't let anyone recognize her. She needed a plan. She could call Dennis on his personal cell phone and have him come to get her... oh, no, she didn't know the number, because it was in her cell phone, which she had left in the limousine. She didn't know any phone numbers any more!

She could take a taxi to her house and trade places with Jane there. She would borrow some of Jane's money from the book in her room, and pay her back when she got home. Yes, that was a good plan. She ran up the steps and went straight to the bookcase... but the book was gone. She searched and searched among the textbook titles, but that one wasn't there. Maybe Jane had hidden money in some other books. She pulled them off the shelf, dusty book by dusty book, and thumbed through the pages of each one, but she didn't find one dollar.

She began to search Jane's room for money. She looked in the classic hiding places, the underwear drawer, but all she found was a bottle of Tylenol hidden under Jane's underclothes. She searched the entire dresser, the desk, the closet, under the mattress, and came up empty. Jane didn't have any money in her room! She hadn't been carrying a purse when they met...so where was her money? She looked in shoes, in socks, in pockets, in every conceivable hiding place, but she didn't find even a dime.

Leeza would have to borrow some money from Sharla. She went into her room and found her purse on the dresser. She quickly opened it and pulled out a twenty-dollar bill, the only money in the purse, then she heard the door slam downstairs. Sharla was home!

Leeza slipped back into Jane's room and wondered how far twenty dollars would take a taxi. Maybe she could call a cab company and ask them. Wait, she didn't even know exactly where she was, how could she even give them directions to come here? Maybe she could walk to a local establishment and then call a taxi from there, and ask them to take her to her house. Oh, no, what was her house number? She never paid attention to it! She hadn't memorized her house number! She lived in Hollywood, on that famous street, but she couldn't even recall the name! She couldn't ask a cab to just take her to Hollywood and then drive her up and down the streets until she found her house. She was stuck here until Jane returned.

However, she didn't have to stay here, in this house. She could go for a walk, wearing the red cloak, and just stay away from the house until this evening. She could buy something to eat with the twenty dollars, and pay back Sharla later. She would let Jane deal with Sharla, and explain why she had left her baby all day. This was not Leeza's problem; this was not Leeza's life.

She waited until she heard Sharla go in the bathroom, and then Leeza silently eased down the steps and out the front door, wearing the red cloak. She ventured in the opposite direction of the house where their mother lived, toward an area that looked like it might have some businesses, a place to get something to eat. She kept her face hidden – she couldn't let anyone recognize her. She just had to get through this day and then she could get back to her own life, her life of luxury and ease; her life without worries.

She found a small, dark coffee shop and made her way to a private booth in the back of the room. She kept her head covered with the hood, even though it was a warm day. A waitress approached her table.

"The special of the day is vegetable beef with barley soup, and avocado-tomato-sprout with cream cheese on wheat," she said.

"That sounds perfect," Leeza said, without making eye contact.

"Jane? Is that you?" the waitress asked.

Leeza didn't know how to answer. If she said yes, she was Jane, then the girl would undoubtedly go into some nostalgic story, or start asking about her family, or who knows what she might want to discuss. If she said no, she wasn't Jane, she might take a closer look and realize she was really Leeza Hamilton, the famous performer. She looked down at the table and didn't look at the waitress.

"You want the soup and sandwich?" she asked, when Leeza didn't reply.

"Yes, please."

"Do you want a whole sandwich, or just half?"

"Half is fine."

"Anything to drink with that?"

"Water. In a bottle."

"One special with a half and a bottle of water, coming right up," she said, as she left the table.

Leeza turned her face to the wall. She didn't want to look at anyone. She didn't want anyone to see her. If she hadn't just ordered lunch, she would leave now, although she was quite hungry. She wondered what kind of delicious meal Hans was preparing for Jane today? Maybe he was fixing a cheese blintz covered with fresh strawberries, and some of his incomparable bubble tea. Maybe he was chopping vegetables for a shrimp salad – or, no, slicing avocados for a taco salad. He knew Leeza loved to have a salad for lunch, and he had recipes for hundreds of different kinds.

She snapped back to the restaurant as her meal was placed before her. Everything smelled delicious... had she eaten today? She was really hungry. She wolfed down the sandwich – ooohhh, that was really tasty, and then she ate the soup, spoonful by loving spoonful. She took a sip of the water, then she decided to take the bottle with her. She needed to get out of this place.

She went to the cash register to pay, and the waitress looked at her oddly. She tried to not notice, but it was so obvious that her eyes were drilling into her. Ignore her, ignore her, she told herself. She didn't know the waitress, and it didn't matter that the waitress thought she knew her. Leeza kept her eyes at a distance, and she left the restaurant as soon as she got her change.

She walked down the street, avoiding all eye contact, feeling like everyone was watching her. Maybe they thought the day was too hot for a red cloak. Maybe she was acting strange. Maybe everyone in this place knew Jane. Maybe they all recognized Leeza.

She had to get away from this business area, and go somewhere that was much more secluded.

The beach would probably be packed on a beautiful day like today. She couldn't go there. She couldn't go back to the house and face Sharla. Where could she go? Could she go back and visit with their mother, now that Sharla was gone? No, she would have to deal with that other lady there, that kind but mysterious stranger.

Nothing was working out the way she had planned. She didn't get to make things right with their mother, she couldn't spend any more time with the baby, and Sharla had turned on her. She just wanted to go back to her own life right now, her wonderful, pampered life! How many hours did she have to wait until it was time to meet Jane?

CHAPTER 15

She found a side street that led to a small park. She passed by many people, probably most of them fans of hers, but she stayed hidden by the red cloak. She sat on the bench of a picnic table for just a few minutes; then a transient-type person sat across from her.

"I know who you are," he said, with a gravelly voice.

Leeza didn't respond.

"I think it's terrible what you did," he said.

What did he think she had done? Did he recognize her as Leeza or Jane?

"You're not going to get away with it forever," he warned.

She didn't have to put up with this kind of behavior. She stood up and began to walk away from the table.

"God knows all about it!" the man shouted. "He's going to give you what you deserve!"

What did he think she deserved? Well, it didn't matter, because this guy had no idea who she was or what she was doing. He was just some crazy guy, and he smelled as if he had been drinking – he didn't even know what he was saying.

Leeza had to go somewhere until tonight, but she had nowhere to go. She was really getting tired – so unlike her; she was always full of energy. Not having her healthy meals prepared for her and not exercising with her personal trainer was already beginning to have an impact on her energy level. She needed to get home and get back on track, so she would be ready for her next performance.

She had to go back to the house. She couldn't stay awake much longer, and she certainly couldn't take a nap anywhere outside of the house. She began to walk in the direction she had originally come, but now she was disoriented. Where was she? The streets and buildings seemed somewhat familiar, but she didn't know the way back to Jane's house. Which way was the beach from here? The sun was almost directly overhead, so it wasn't helping her sense of direction. The heat of the day and the warm cloak were rapidly draining her energy. Still, she had to force herself to keep going.

Where was that coffee shop? Where was that street? Her steps were slowing as she rounded a corner of another place she didn't recognize. She should know this area, but it looked all so strange to her. She dragged her feet, fearing she would collapse at any time and then, all of a sudden, there was Jane's house, right in front of her. She walked up to the porch and silently let herself in the front door. She paused before crossing the room to listen for voices or sounds of movement. She didn't hear anyone – had Sharla left for work? – so she slithered up the steps and fell across Jane's bed, without even bothering to remove the red cloak. She just needed to close her eyes for a few minutes, or for a few hours.

CHAPTER 16

When she awakened, she kept still for several minutes, trying to determine if anyone else was at home. She didn't hear anyone: no baby noises, no one in the kitchen bumping pots and pans, no one in the shower or anywhere in the house. She looked at the clock – she had a few hours before it was time to meet Jane – and she decided to get something to eat. She took off the cloak and quietly went down the steps, still listening, and into the kitchen.

Something drew her out of the kitchen and into the small office, which was off the living room. She felt as if she needed to know about a specific thing that was in the office. She looked at the wall of bookshelves... no, that wasn't it. She sat at the desk, thinking how odd it was that they didn't have a computer. She opened the center drawer and was delighted to see the variety of pens. She was almost inspired to draw a picture and use every one of the colors, but she really didn't have time for that right now. She opened the top drawer on the right and found several different colors of stamp pads, and all kinds of stamps. What did they do with all these stamps? Did someone actually have a hobby of stamping imprints on paper? She closed the drawer and, with some difficulty, she opened the drawer below it. It was packed with folders full of papers.

What was all this stuff? Her eyes felt like they wanted to blur, because there was just too much stuff in this drawer to comprehend. There were ticket stubs, receipts, instruction booklets, envelopes, advertisements, lists, recipes, newspaper clippings... didn't they ever put anything in the garbage? Did they save every piece of paper they received?

As Leeza attempted to get everything back into the drawer so she could close it, several of the newspaper clippings fell to the floor. She was about to put them into their proper folder when the one on top caught her attention.

'Teenager Not Guilty of Murder, Declared Insane,' the headline read. Leeza read the article about a 17-year-old girl who killed her father with a fireplace poker while trying to protect her sister. She was found to be unable to stand trial, and she was sent to a mental hospital. Her name wasn't mentioned in the article, probably because she was a minor, Leeza figured. She found several other articles that added a few more details to the story: the girl had accused her father of abusing her, and she felt she had to protect her sister; the sister, who was 16, refused to speak to anyone about anything; their mother had a mental breakdown after the incident; investigations were continuing.

The whole scenario seemed oddly familiar to Leeza. She vaguely remembered watching a movie based on this incident. The movie had really over-dramatized the whole situation, and Leeza had stopped watching it when she saw all the blood, that awful red blood, all over the house when the girl killed her father. She had not seen the part about the mental breakdowns. She shuddered when she recalled that movie. It had really made an impact on her; she was recalling the scenes too vividly. She had to put it out of her mind. She did not ever again want to watch any kind of movie that included blood or terror. She preferred light-hearted love stories or family adventure movies.

None of the clippings had dates on them, but they were all slightly yellow, so Leeza figured they were old. Why did Sharla and Jane have these articles in their office? Obviously, they saved all kinds of things, but why this?

CHAPTER 17

Leeza heard the front door opening, so she stuffed all the folders back into the drawer and, with great effort, was able to get the drawer closed. She turned away from the desk, feeling like she had been caught with her hand in the cookie jar, but Sharla didn't see her. She passed by the office with Shari – beautiful, delicate Shari, who looked right at Leeza – in her arms and carried her up the steps. Leeza wanted to avoid Sharla, so she kept quiet and decided to not get anything to eat right now. She could wait until she got back home and she would ask Hans to fix something special for her. Everything Hans fixed for her was special, so she would not be asking him for anything out of the ordinary.

She returned to Jane's room and softly closed the door. She had nothing else to say to Sharla. That was Jane's territory now. What a relief, just knowing that in a few short hours she would be back to her own life, her real life, her normal, extraordinary life as one of the beautiful people, loved and adored by millions. She relaxed on the bed as she pictured her house, her staff, her own life, looking forward to her regular routine.

Leeza sat up straight in bed, in the darkness. What time was it? She slipped down the steps, then she remembered that she had forgotten the red cloak. She noiselessly sneaked back up the steps, went into Jane's bedroom, grabbed the cloak and was able to get out the door without awakening Sharla and Shari. Oh, she hadn't said goodbye to Shari. Well, she didn't have time now, she was probably already late. She put on the cloak as she went out the back door and hurried down the steps to the beach, almost falling twice. She ran with great difficulty in the cloak, all the way to the spot where she was to meet Jane. She rested by the huge driftwood log, peering into the darkness. She didn't see anyone at all. She hoped she wasn't too late… but no, Jane would wait for her. Last night, Jane was desperate to have her own life back – and now Leeza was, too.

After resting for a few minutes, she was energized, anxious to find Jane. She could not stay still. She paced around the beach, going down to the water and back to the brush, up and down the sandy dunes, watching and waiting, but she didn't see her anywhere. Tonight the moon was filtered by some high clouds, so the night was a lot darker than last night. Where could Jane be?

Leeza was losing patience. She had had enough of this life, Jane's plain, complicated life. She didn't care if her own life didn't have any meaning; it was her life and she loved it. She just needed to get back to it, right now.

She began heading for the parking lot where Dennis had left her the other night... was that only two nights ago? It seemed as if a lifetime had passed since she arrived here, maybe two lifetimes. Her own bed, her staff, her delicious meals, her swimming pool were now but memories, so long ago it was almost as if she had dreamed them. Hans and Gretchen, Karman and Kelly, Nita and Dennis, and especially Chad... where were they now? She had to get back to the luxury and comfort of her own life.

She reached the parking lot, which was empty except for an old VW bus in the corner, which looked like it had been sitting there for months. Where was Dennis with her limousine? She sat on a large rock where she could see the entire parking lot, waiting for the slightest sound that would signal that a car was approaching. The night was calm and quiet.

Perhaps Jane had misunderstood her instructions, and she was going to be arriving late. The traffic coming out of Hollywood could be bad; there could have been an accident on the freeway. Leeza could be early – she hadn't even checked the time before she left the house; or Leeza could be so late that she had missed the meeting time, and Jane had decided not to wait for her. Maybe Jane was having so much fun in Leeza's life, she didn't want to come home to her own life. What if Leeza had to stay here forever? No, that would be ridiculous. It would be impossible! All she would have to do was tell someone who she really was, then Dennis would come and get her. Her staff wouldn't let her stay away – they couldn't exist without her.

She became aware that a car was approaching the parking lot. She slipped into the bushes to hide herself. A small car – was it red? – pulled into the parking lot and stopped just a short distance away from her. Had Jane asked someone else to bring her here?

Two young men got out of the car and sat on the hood. They huddled around something and Leeza suspected that they were doing something with some kind of drugs. She felt as if she knew who they were, but she couldn't risk being seen. They laughed and spoke quietly to each other. Leeza wanted to get away from them, but she knew if she made even the slightest movement, the bushes would reveal her hiding place. She waited, impatiently, for them to leave. They seemed to be staying quite a long time, just sitting on the hood and doing secret deeds in the dark.

After what seemed like an hour, they finally got back into their little car and left. Leeza came out of the bushes and again sat on the rock for a few minutes. Why was Jane so late? Where could she be? Didn't she realize the importance of their meeting tonight? Jane had to come home to her baby and she had to let Leeza have her own life back again.

How could she get a message to Jane? She couldn't call her – Leeza didn't even know her own phone number, which was kept private. She hadn't paid any attention to her address, since she had other people to take care of all the details of her life. She couldn't even call any of those other people, her staff or her manager, since their numbers were all in her cell phone which Jane had right now.

Her mind was going in circles. She kept reviewing the same information, somehow expecting to come up with different results. All she could do was to wait for Jane. She didn't like being put in this position. She needed to be the one in control of the situation. She needed to be the director of the show. Other people needed to be waiting for her. Nobody kept Leeza Hamilton waiting! How dare Jane take advantage of her like this! She should know better than to leave the famous Leeza Hamilton in the dark, in the middle of the night, all night! Oh, why didn't she have a watch? The night was passing and Jane still wasn't here.

Leeza began pacing back and forth in the parking lot. Jane had to be coming, where was Jane? Jane had to be coming, where was Jane? Jane had to be coming, where was Jane? Her steps seemed to be chanting this phrase, taunting Leeza. Leeza couldn't take it any more. She couldn't wait any longer. What were her options? She didn't have any! All she could do was wait! What could she do, now that she couldn't wait? She could wait here or she could wait on the beach. Neither was a doable choice. She had to get away from here – not just away from this parking lot, but also away from this whole life! She had to get back home!

She was tired of pacing, tired of standing, tired of being here, tired of being awake. The entire night had passed – the landscape was beginning to come into view with the morning light. Leeza could not stay here any longer. She would have to return to Jane's house and get some sleep. If Jane had had a problem so that she couldn't leave Leeza's house – maybe Dennis had a situation with his wife and couldn't drive her, or maybe Jane had fallen asleep and missed her opportunity to leave the house last night – Jane would know where to find Leeza. She would not be able to stay away from her own baby for long. She could just come home and they would trade places there. Leeza could stay in Jane's room, unseen by Sharla, and when Jane arrived and came up to her room then Leeza could leave. Yes, Jane would know what to do.

How Leeza longed for a good night's sleep in her own king-size bed! However, right now, she would settle for Jane's bed, seemingly so far away, such a long distance up the beach. She walked and walked, dragging her feet in the sand. She usually enjoyed this first morning time, so quiet and still, before the rest of the world was awake, but after last night, which had been such a long night, she could not take any pleasure in the fresh morning now. She didn't have any energy. She needed sleep and she needed food; she was more tired than hungry, so she would go straight to bed, then get up later and eat something.

After an extremely long and tiring walk to Jane's house, Leeza almost didn't have the energy to climb the steps from the beach up to the house. She had to force each step, coaxing her legs to cooperate with her mind that so desperately needed to rest. She just had to get inside the house, to Jane's room, just a few more steps. She felt as if she would fall asleep if she just stopped walking for a second, so she didn't let herself stop until she reached Jane's bed. She fell into a deep sleep as soon as her head touched the pillow.

CHAPTER 18

What should have been a relaxing and refreshing rest was ruined by a horrible nightmare. Leeza's mind replayed that movie she had seen of the murder documented in the newspaper clippings she read yesterday, adding to it a few unsettling scenes. She tried to shake the scenes from her mind, but they seemed to be stuck there, wanting her to review them again and again.

She watched herself enter an older, large house, a familiar house, one she had seen on TV many times, with a grand staircase leading to the upper floors just inside the front door. She heard a muffled crying sound coming from one of the upstairs room, sounds of things bumping against the wall or floor. She saw herself walking up the steps, as if she were watching herself in a play. She then was coming into a room, a dark, green room, where a man was hurting a woman. The woman was crying; her clothes were torn. Leeza was so confused as to what was happening; she thought she knew these people, and they should not be doing this, they should not even be here. The man was large and the woman was small; he was on her and she was crying.

The woman's face transformed into a girl's face – it was Sharla's face, when she was just a girl. Her eyes were closed; she was in great pain. She didn't see Leeza, and neither did the man, who was wholly focused on his task. Leeza grabbed a poker from beside the fireplace – this old house had a fireplace in almost every room – and she hit the man on the back of his head, to make him stop hurting Sharla. He immediately stopped moving and fell to the ground. Bright red blood was all over the room, on the walls, on the floor, everywhere. Leeza backed out of the room and ran down the steps, surrounded by splatters of blood throughout the house. She couldn't stand the color of blood! The red was so painful!

Leeza began to run as soon as she was out of the house, then she awakened in Jane's bed, her heart pounding. She hated that dream! Why had she ever watched that movie, just so it could come back to haunt her? Why did she have to come to this house, to look in that room, to find that article, to remind her of that awful incident? She never wanted to have that dream again! All she wanted was to get back to her own life, her Hollywood life of luxury, and get away from this place!

CHAPTER 19

She wondered what time it was. She wondered what day it was. How many days had she been here, in Jane's house? She had waited all night for Jane, but was that last night or the night before last night? She was losing track of time. She knew she needed to be back in her own life by Saturday, because that was the night of her next concert, but she wasn't sure what day was today. In her own house, she could ask any of her staff what day it was. They were always happy to help her with everything, and they understood that she didn't concern herself with details, such as numbers or figures or days or times. They took care of all the particulars for her, so she could concentrate on taking the best care of herself, for the sake of her career, as well as their own livelihoods.

Leeza was really hungry. How long had it been since she had eaten? Was Sharla at home? Leeza would have to risk a confrontation with Sharla, because she needed food, right now. She was still wearing the red cloak, so she took it off and hung it in Jane's closet. She had been wearing these clothes for a long time. She should find something else to wear. She could use a shower. Well, all that would have to wait, because she needed to eat before she could do anything else.

She went down to the kitchen where Sharla was feeding Shari. Oh, how she had missed Shari! She could not imagine how much Jane must miss her. Leeza focused her attention on that cute little face with the chubby cheeks, the big eyes concentrating on Sharla, as if she were her mother. How could Jane just abandon her daughter like this? If Sharla weren't here, Jane never could have left Shari for these few days. But then, if Sharla weren't here, Jane would not have been on the beach to meet Leeza the other night. Jane would have had to stay home; she couldn't have left the house at night. Then Leeza would have just returned to Dennis waiting at her limo, and to her own life. She would not have had this opportunity to explore what might be a meaning to life. Since everything happened for a reason, she must be here now for a reason.

"So you finally decided to rejoin the land of the living?" Sharla asked, breaking into Leeza's private thoughts.

Leeza's head snapped over to look at Sharla. She didn't know what to say to her.

"Yeah, I'm hungry," she responded.

"It's all about you," Sharla said. "Open up, big bite," she said to Shari.

"Where do you work?" Leeza asked, as the question popped into her head.

"As if you care anything about me," Sharla said.

"I do!" Leeza insisted. Jane must care about her own sister.

"There's some French toast on the stove," Sharla said, uninterested in anything Leeza had to say.

Leeza turned to the stove and put two slices of French toast on a plate. She looked for some jam – she preferred raspberry jam on her French toast – but she didn't see any, so she settled for maple syrup. She was a little disgusted to see on the package that the flavor was artificial, but she was so hungry right now, she would have to settle for what she could get. She poured a glass of orange juice (from concentrate!) and sat at the table beside Shari. She realized she didn't have a fork, so she got one out of the sink, washed it, and returned to her seat at the table.

"Not that you might in any way care about anyone but yourself, but Mom hasn't come back since you were there," Sharla said accusingly. "Her nurse said she's slipping into a coma. They might have to put in a feeding tube, because she won't eat."

"It's not my fault," Leeza said defensively.

"Why is it always about you?" Sharla asked. "No one said it was your fault."

"I just—"

"Let me finish!" Sharla interrupted. "I don't think she's going to live much longer, so we need to make some decisions."

"Decisions?" Leeza asked.

"Yeah, about her funeral, if she should stay on life support, those kinds of things."

Leeza didn't want to think about those kinds of things, much less talk about them. "Let's talk about it tomorrow," she said. Jane would be back home by then.

"We can't always put everything off until tomorrow!" Sharla said. She seemed to be really irritated. "If you want to waive your authority, I'll just take care of it," she said, then she mumbled, "like I always do."

Leeza wondered what was the matter with Jane. Sharla did seem to be taking care of everything. She was the one with the job. She took care of Shari and all her needs. Her part of the household was in order, while Jane's room was in disarray. Jane really had some kind of problem with taking responsibility. What was Jane's problem? She wished she could ask Sharla, but then she would be giving away their secret.

"We can talk about it now, then," Leeza said reluctantly.

"Forget it. I'll just make all the decisions," Sharla said.

"No, really, what's to decide?" Leeza took a small bite. It had no flavor.

"We want to respect Mom's wishes," Sharla said.

"Yeah, sure, of course, obviously."

"She told me before, she doesn't want to be on life support."

"Okay, no life support." Leeza took a sip of the juice. It tasted sour. Her appetite was gone.

"But she didn't really say anything about a feeding tube. I don't really consider that life support, do you? Because it could be just a temporary condition. She could come out of the comatose state. What do you think about that?"

"I agree," Leeza said. She didn't want to think about it at all.

"She wants to be buried, not cremated," Sharla said.

"Buried it shall be," Leeza said.

"But you know that will be a lot more expensive, the casket and the cemetery plot and everything."

Leeza did not know that. She didn't ever think about death, much less the expenses associated with death. She did know that she had a huge insurance policy on her own life, but did regular people have life insurance?

"And one more thing," Sharla said tentatively.

"What?"

"She told me, a long time ago, she wants to be buried by Dad."

That sounded logical. Leeza wondered how and when their dad had died.

"Okay," Leeza agreed, as Sharla closely watched her reaction. What was she expecting from her?

"You're okay with that?" Sharla asked. "I mean, you're not just saying that?"

"Why wouldn't I be okay with that?" Leeza asked. "A wife should be buried next to her husband."

Sharla stared at her. Leeza felt that she had said something wrong, she had made some mistake. Sharla now must know that she wasn't Jane, because, for some reason, Jane didn't want their mother to be buried next to their father. When Leeza blinked her eyes, the bright red blood splotches were lingering behind her eyelids. She opened her eyes wide and looked at Shari, to erase those images.

"I never thought I would hear you say that," Sharla finally responded, "at least, not about Mom and Dad."

Leeza wondered what she meant by that. She thought about the fact that there were no photographs of their father in the house. He must have been out of the picture for quite some time.

"Well, I'm saying it now," Leeza said. "She should get what she wants in death, even if she isn't getting it in life."

"How dare you!" Sharla shouted.

"Do you think she wants this kind of life?"

"Not everyone can just do whatever they want, like you!"

"But she didn't choose this kind of life!"

"No, she didn't! And I have been doing everything I can, every day, to try to make things better for her, as good as they can possibly be, in her condition. You haven't ever done anything to help her!"

"I—" she didn't know what to say, since she really hadn't been there to do anything. Apparently Jane hadn't helped her at all.

"I'm sorry," Sharla said, her voice softening. "Just forget I said that. I didn't mean it. Are you okay?"

"Yeah... I'm... fine," Leeza answered, curious about this new tone of voice, this changed attitude of Sharla's.

"Okay, just take it easy. Do you want something else to eat? Are you still hungry? I can make you a smoothie, if you want, or I can fry you a couple of eggs. Hey, we have some hash browns in the freezer. You love hash browns!"

Leeza was still hungry, but now she was even more curious about Sharla's sudden change of manner. Maybe if she stayed at the table, eating, Sharla would reveal why she was acting this way and what she meant.

"Sounds good," Leeza said.

"Eggs or hash browns?" Sharla asked, setting aside Shari's spoon, standing, and going over to the refrigerator.

"They both sound good."

"Okay, two fried eggs, over easy, just how you like them, on top of a pile of shredded hash browns, your favorite."

"Yummy," Leeza said, just for something to say. She didn't really like fried eggs, and she hoped the hash browns wouldn't be fried. What was with America's obsession with frying all the good food and thus removing all the goodness? She watched Sharla take out the cooking oil – she didn't even use olive oil – and pour too much of it into a frying pan. She turned to Shari, so she didn't have to see how her food was being prepared. Did Sharla cook all the meals around here? What did Jane do with all her time, anyway?

Shari burped and a stream of baby food flowed out of her little mouth. Leeza was in the process of getting a napkin when Sharla quickly reached between Leeza and Shari, and wiped the brown mush off her face with her bib. In one motion, she removed the bib and Shari was once again the model baby. Shari smiled at Leeza, reaching out for her. Leeza pointed her finger so Shari could grab it. She tried to pull it into her mouth, but that was where Leeza drew the line; her hand wasn't entering a baby's mouth.

"Here ya go," Sharla said, placing a plate of food in front of Leeza.

"Wow, all this?" There was enough food to feed a family of four.

"I know how hungry you get."

"Wow," Leeza said, not wanting to eat this fried stack of food. It did smell good, though.

Sharla sat down at her place at the table and watched Leeza.

"Do you want some of this?" Leeza asked. "I can't eat all this."

"No, I already ate. You go ahead."

"So, what were we talking about?" Leeza asked, in an attempt to get the conversation going again. She took a small bite as Sharla watched intently.

"What were we talking about?" Sharla asked, avoiding the subject.

"Oh, yeah, we were talking about Mom's wishes," Leeza said.

"Oh, yeah, that's right," Sharla faked remembering. "Well, that's about it. She doesn't have a will, as far as I know, but she has some insurance, and that should cover her final expenses."

"Well, that's good," Leeza said. How could she stimulate more conversation, to get Sharla to really talk to her, without letting her know she wasn't Jane?

"So, I'm going to tell them tomorrow to put in the feeding tube," Sharla said.

"Oh, yeah, right," Leeza said.

"You're gonna need one if you don't eat," Sharla warned.

"I'm eating!"

"Um... I heard you go out last night," Sharla said.

"You did?" Leeza replied. She had no idea how Jane would react to that statement. Was it okay if she went out at night?

"Yeah. Did you go walking again?"

"Yes." That was a question she could answer, as Jane or Leeza.

"How long were you gone? I didn't hear you come back in."

"Not too long," she lied. Leeza was curious about this life, but she was not curious enough about it to forget about her own life, her wonderful life. She was just staying here until Jane returned, and at the moment she did return, Leeza would be gone, far away from here.

"I really don't like you walking around after dark," Sharla said.

"Why not? It's so peaceful, and I didn't see anyone else," she said, as she thought, unfortunately, because she should have seen Jane. She didn't consider the two boys to be anyone.

"Make sure no one else sees you," Sharla warned.

CHAPTER 20

Leeza raised an eyebrow. Why shouldn't anyone see Jane?

"You really should just stay here, and not be walking around. Did you wear the cloak?" Sharla asked.

"Yes," Leeza said. Leeza knew why it was important to her to wear the cloak... why would it be important to Sharla for Jane to wear it?

"Oh, good. I know you know, but I just don't want you to forget."

What would Jane forget? Why did she need to wear the cloak when she went for a walk?

"I won't forget," Leeza assured her.

"Just don't go out tonight, okay?"

"Why not?"

"You know. It's too risky. Just stay in the house tonight."

Why did Sharla want to keep Jane as a prisoner in her own house? Leeza couldn't stay here tonight: she had to go out, to meet Jane. Surely Jane would have Dennis bring her back tonight, and she and Leeza would trade places, and each would be back in her regular life. Oh, how Leeza longed to return to her regular life! Why had she ever thought this would be a good idea, trading places with Jane, anyway?

Sharla took Shari to the living room and put her in the playpen.

"I'm going to go see Mom again, but I don't think you should go see her any more."

"Yeah, whatever," Leeza replied. She didn't care any more about finishing old business – she just wanted to finish her stay here at Jane's house.

"So I'm going to leave Shari here with you," Sharla said. "Is that okay? Do you mind? I mean, are you okay with that? I won't be gone long."

"No, that's fine," Leeza said. She hoped Jane would return while Sharla was gone, so Leeza could go back home, where she belonged. She felt so out of place here, so stifled, so uncomfortable. "She didn't seem to know me anyway."

"Glad to see you are yourself again," Sharla remarked.

"What do you mean by that?"

"Nothing, you are just yourself again."

"What? What do you mean?"

"Well, for a couple of days, you were suddenly interested in Mom. I still can't believe you went to see her yesterday, after all this time. I mean, that's a good thing. But it just seemed so odd, so out of character for you. I never thought you would change your mind. Usually when you say you'll never do something, you stick to your decision forever."

"Out of character, yeah, that's how I feel," Leeza admitted.

"No, I mean you *were* out of character, but you are back to normal now, I mean, normal for you, your usual self."

"Oh." Leeza didn't know what else to say to that. She didn't want to be in character for Jane, she wanted to be in her own character in her own home, in her own life. How could she be Jane's usual self?

"Well, I'm on my way," Sharla said, as she went out the front door.

Leeza didn't know what to do. At this time of day, she should have finished with her personal trainer, and either be swimming, relaxing in her hot tub, or having a massage, giving Hans suggestions on what she would like to have for dinner. She looked forward to being back in her house – could she be there by dinnertime tonight? How could she make that happen? Why didn't she even know her own cell phone number, so she could call Jane?

She felt like her mind was going in circles. She had already thought of every possible solution, every possible way home, and none of them were possible. She watched Shari chew on a block for a few minutes and she couldn't understand how Jane could have left her own daughter, even for one day. Yes, Leeza had been extremely persuasive, but Jane should have stood her ground. She should have insisted that they couldn't trade places. What kind of mother was she, anyway?

On the other hand, maybe Jane was a deeply involved mother who really needed a break from her baby, and Leeza's offer was too good to refuse: a chance to get away from it all, to be pampered for a day. However, she was taking it too far now; she was taking advantage of this situation by leaving Leeza here in her life for too long.

Leeza wandered out to the deck and watched the ocean, waving, waving, waving at her. Each wave was unique; not one went the exact same way or in the exact same place as the wave before it. She was mesmerized by the motion, paralyzed by the beauty, awed by the expanse. The ocean flowed as far as she could see, to the north, to the south, to the west. It was remarkable how so much moving water stopped at the coastline... why didn't it overflow and just keep coming this way, and cover this whole town? How did it stay within its boundaries, without a wall to hold it?

Why hadn't she stayed within her own boundaries? Why did she have to go and do something out of the ordinary, just because she didn't have a wall to hold her? She had done it just because she wanted to do it. That was the difference between her and the ocean – she had free will to do whatever she chose to do, and the ocean had to do whatever God told it to do.

She felt like she had a remarkable awakening, but she didn't get it. It didn't make sense. The ocean was still doing what it should be doing, and she was doing something she didn't want to be doing, in a place she didn't want to be. Could she rightfully come to the conclusion that if she had stayed within her boundaries, like the ocean did, then she would still be doing what she wanted to be doing in a place she wanted to be?

Leeza was growing more and more uncomfortable at this house, in this life. Something was really stinky about Jane's life. Was she just avoiding her responsibilities, or was she truly a mental case? An unsettling thought occurred to Leeza. Could it be possible that Jane did have mental problems, and she now thought she was really Leeza? What if she had adopted Leeza's lifestyle, just like that, and was now planning to stay where she was, forever? No, that was not possible, because Jane would never be able to perform on stage like Leeza. She didn't know the songs, she didn't know the dance moves, she didn't have the stage presence that Leeza had. There was no way on earth that Jane could step into Leeza's life and do all the things Leeza did. Actually, Leeza was surprised that Dennis or Karman or Kelly or Nita hadn't realized by now that Jane wasn't Leeza. If they were spending any time with her, the truth would be revealed.

Shari's cry brought Leeza back to the here and now, the reality of Jane's life. She ran into the house, banging the door behind her, to see what was the matter with Shari. Leeza stopped short when she saw blood all over the playpen! Shari was crying and Leeza was frozen in place. The splatters of blood brought back the memory of her dream, of that movie, and she was petrified. Why was there so much blood everywhere? How did the blood get all over the house? It wasn't her fault! She didn't do it! She just wanted to stop the crying!

CHAPTER 21

Leeza heard a loud scream, which shocked her. Who else was in the house? She could not move, she was so scared. She saw hands reaching for Shari, yet unable to reach her, unable to comfort her. The bright red of the blood was a stop sign to Leeza. Her body would not respond to the commands her brain was giving. She had to do something, she had to do something, she didn't know what to do! She didn't know how to fix this! Why wouldn't the baby stop crying?

The front door flew open and Sharla ran into the house.

"I heard a scream! What's the matter? What happened? WHAT'S GOING ON?"

Leeza could hear what Sharla was saying but could not think of the way to get her tongue to respond; nor could she think of an answer. She didn't know!

"Oh, my baby, what's the matter?" Sharla asked, leaning into the playpen to gather Shari into her arms. Shari calmed her cry into a whimper as she buried her head on Sharla's shoulder.

Leeza decided the scream must have been her own; but why was so much blood all over the room, everywhere she looked?

"Oh, oh, I see," Sharla said with relief. "Your nose is bleeding," she said to Shari. "Let's go get you cleaned up and change your clothes." She took Shari upstairs.

As Leeza regained her senses, she realized the blood was, in fact, not all over the room, but just in blotches in the playpen. She felt like she should make some effort to clean it up, but she had no idea how to do it. Wasn't blood some odd substance that needed a special cleaner? She felt sick to her stomach; she could not continue to look at the red blood any longer. The color red itself was upsetting to her, but the sight of blood took her over the edge. She had to leave the room. She rushed into the bathroom and thought she was going to vomit – but she didn't. She washed her face and hands in hot water, dried them well, and looked at herself in the mirror.

Leeza felt the utmost urgency that she must leave this house as soon as possible! She would find a way back to her own house. Dennis had maybe driven for about two hours when he brought her here... but that was from the house where the party was held, which was not anywhere near her house. Since she didn't drive, she never paid attention to directions or street names or locations. She may as well be as far away as China – that was on the other side of the world, was it not? – for the help her lack of navigation skills would be in getting her home.

She had an idea. She could put on the red cloak, and then find her way to the highway, and then she could hitchhike to Hollywood. Once she arrived in Hollywood, it should be easy to find her neighborhood and her house. She didn't have to worry about anyone hurting her – when she got in the car, she would pull down the cloak to reveal her true identity. Everybody loved her, so whoever the driver turned out to be would be anxious to help her get back home.

Yes, this was a good plan. The parking lot where Dennis had left her must be near the highway. She would go down the beach, up to the parking lot, and follow the road to the highway.

She was excited and relieved at the same time. She was regaining some control! Finally, she would be getting away from this place, and she could get back to her own life! She really didn't care about what happened here, in Jane's life. She felt as if she had discovered the meaning of her life: to stay within her own boundaries, to follow her own schedule, to perform and make people happy, like Karman had said, so very long ago, the other night after her performance.

She scurried up the steps to Jane's room to get the red cloak. She heard Sharla talking in a high voice to Shari as she quietly grabbed the cloak and went back down the stairs. She stepped out onto the back deck and put on the cloak. She quickly went down the wooden steps to the beach, moving as quickly as she could, with the cloak making it difficult to go as fast as she wanted to go. She couldn't take off Jane's shoes now to enjoy the hot sand, but she smiled at the thought of it. As much as she loved the beach, this was not the life for her.

Soon she was at the parking lot. She decided to slow her pace so as not to arouse suspicion. Wouldn't people think it strange to see a cloaked figure running in this area, especially one wearing a red cloak? A person in a black cloak might not draw as much attention, but a red cloak couldn't be dismissed.

She walked down the street, looking for a sign pointing to the highway, or anything she recognized. This area did not seem in any way familiar to her– but it had been dark when they arrived the other night, and she hadn't been paying much attention to her surroundings at that time. She thought the streets were strangely deserted – didn't anyone walk or drive around here? She stopped to listen for a moment, to listen for any sounds of life. All she could hear was her own pounding heart. Where were the dogs, the kids, the people, the cars? This place was really very isolated.

After standing still for a few moments, she could hear some sounds of traffic to her right. She went right on the next street and soon came to a sign directing her to the highway. She was almost there! She was pretty sure hitchhiking was legal here, in this state and in this county. In just a couple of hours, she would be home!

She walked onto the shoulder of the on-ramp, deciding exactly where to stand. She found a good spot near a signpost, stopped, and turned to face the coming traffic. Her new problem was that no cars were coming. Had she been in a ghost town? No, of course not, because she had been in Jane's house with Sharla and Shari, she had gone to the house where their mother was, and she had seen people in the coffee shop, not to mention those two guys she had seen doing drugs in the parking lot. The town was just sleepy, it wasn't deserted.

A red car turned onto the on-ramp and Leeza suddenly panicked. It looked just like the car she had seen in the parking lot, the one with the two drug addicts in it! She was relieved when it passed by her without stopping to offer her a ride. Then she realized that she didn't have her thumb in the hitchhiking position; maybe they didn't know she wanted a ride. She stuck up her thumb when she heard another car approaching. Again, this car drove right by her. She considered lowering the cloak hood so her face could be seen. If people knew who she really was, they would be eager to take her, the famous Leeza Hamilton, any place she wanted to go.

Another car was coming slowly down the on-ramp, and Leeza was anxious for a second. She didn't want to ride with strangers. She lowered her thumb and stuck her hand in the cloak pocket. She would have to find another way to get home; this was not a good option.

The car, a large car with tinted windows, stopped beside her and the passenger window was lowered.

CHAPTER 22

"Do you need a ride?" the driver asked. He was an older man – older than she was, anyway. He could be an ax murderer!

"No, I'm just waiting for someone," she said.

"Come on, I'll take you home," he said.

"No, thank you." She stepped away from the car.

"You don't have to worry about anything."

"No, thanks." She began walking back towards the road, away from the highway.

The driver put the car into reverse and followed her, going backwards.

"Come on, just get in the car."

"No, really, I'll just walk."

"I'm not going to hurt you. I'm a police officer. I'll take you home," he said kindly.

Leeza took a good look at the car and the driver. The car didn't have any police emblems on it. Inside the car was a barrier between the front and back seats. She saw a police radio and one of those fancy police computers. He flashed a badge, but she was still hesitant to get in the car with him.

"I don't think so," Leeza said. She was uncomfortable with the whole situation. Why didn't Dennis come to get her?

"You need to get in the car. Come on. You can ride in the front seat. You are not under arrest or anything. I just don't want you walking out here, so close to the highway."

"Can you give me a ride to my house?" she asked.

"Yes, of course."

"All the way?"

"Sure. Come on. Get in. We're blocking traffic."

One car was behind the police car on the on-ramp.

"Are you a sheriff?" she asked. Somehow it was important for her to know that.

"Yes, I am a sheriff." He showed her his badge again, and she noticed it was in the shape of a star. He must indeed be a sheriff.

"Are you allowed to cross county lines?"

"In the line of duty, yes, miss, I am allowed to cross county lines."

Leeza considered her options, or lack of them, and she decided this would be a safe way for her to get home – as a matter of fact, the only way for her to get home. She opened the passenger door.

"Can I open this door from the inside?" she asked.

"Of course. Like I said, you are not a prisoner. I'm just going to give you a ride home." He smiled at her, a comforting smile.

"Oh, thank God!" she said, sitting in the passenger seat. She closed the door and pulled the hood of the cloak off her head as the sheriff pulled onto the freeway.

"Buckle up," he said.

"Of course, you know who I am?" she asked, expecting a great reaction when he realized he had the famous Leeza Hamilton in his car.

"Of course, I know who you are," he said, nodding. He pulled the car microphone to his mouth and said something in code that she didn't understand, then he replaced the microphone.

"So, I live in Hollywood," Leeza said. "I'm not sure of the exact address, but once we get there, I can show you where it is," she said, in an effort to convince herself that she could indeed find her house.

"Okay," he said. "So, what are you doing here?"

"I was just visiting someone," she said.

"Oh, really?" he asked. "Who were you visiting?"

"Oh, you probably don't know them," she said.

"Well, there's a good chance I do," he said. "I know most of the people around here. I just live not too far from here, and it's my business to know the people in the county."

"Well, these are very private people and they don't know many other people," she said. That sounded logical to her.

"Oh, I see," he said. "Maybe you're right. Maybe I don't know them."

They drove down the highway for about 20 minutes when the sheriff turned on an exit.

"What are you doing?" Leeza asked. "This isn't the Hollywood exit."

"I know, I just have to go this way," he said. "Don't worry, I'll have you home in no time."

Leeza began to get scared. Where was he taking her? She thought about getting out of the car when he slowed to a stop. She didn't want to ride with him any more. She didn't trust him.

"I need to get some gas," he said, "then we'll get back on the highway."

Leeza thought the police got their gas at a special place, so she was surprised when he turned into a regular gas station. She was more surprised when he pulled up next to the full-service pump. She didn't even know any gas stations still offered full service.

He purchased five dollars worth of gasoline, the attendant pumped it, and then the sheriff drove around a big loop to get back on the highway. Leeza relaxed, almost laughing to herself because she had nearly panicked a few minutes ago. She was going to be home in just a matter of minutes, or at the most, an hour or so.

She stared out the window as they continued on their route. The palm trees were blowing in the wind. The day was sunny and beautiful. She almost felt sleepy in the warm car as she watched the scenery, the hundreds of mini-malls that lined the highway. She searched for the ocean – she loved to see it whenever she was riding along the coastline, but they must have made that turn that brought them farther inland, because she could no longer see the water.

She couldn't think of anything to say to the sheriff, so they rode in silence for a short while. He hadn't told her his name... was he wearing a nametag? The police usually did. She turned to look at him and realized that something didn't look right. She looked out his window to let her mind comprehend... they were going north! She could see the ocean through the driver's window!

CHAPTER 23

"Where are we going?" she demanded.

"I'm taking you home," he said calmly.

"No, I want to go to MY home," she explained.

"We are going to your home." He nodded toward the highway.

"We aren't going the right way."

"Yes, we are. I know the way."

"This is not the way to Hollywood," she said, pointing ahead.

"I know the way to your house."

"You know where I live?"

"Yes, I do." He glanced in her direction.

"You know my exact address?"

"Yes, I do."

"How do you know where I live?"

"I've been there before, many times."

"What are you talking about?" She shook her head slightly, trying to make sense of what he was saying.

"Come on, Jane, stop playing games. You know who I am, Officer Jon Stiles. You've known me all your life."

He knew Jane, and he thought she was Jane! He was taking her back to Jane's house!

"No, I'm not Jane. I'm Leeza Hamilton. Don't you recognize me? You know, the singer? Everybody knows me!"

"Yeah, sure, Jane, Leeza, Matilda, whoever you are today," he said, shrugging his shoulders. "This is getting kind of old."

"What?"

"I said, this is getting kind of old."

"I know what you said, but what do you mean? What are you talking about?"

"You need to be more careful and stay closer to home."

"That's what I'm trying to do! I'm trying to get home!"

"And so I'm taking you home," he concluded.

"No! I'm not Jane! Don't take me to Jane's house! My house is in Hollywood! I live in Hollywood!"

"So today it's Hollywood, huh? Last week it was Denver."

"No, really, I'm not Jane! Look at me! We sort of look alike, but she is... well, plain, and I'm famous!"

"That's a good one." He chuckled lightly.

"No, really! I just did a concert the other night, and then I came and traded places with Jane! She's at my house right now, and I need to get back there, so she can come home to her daughter."

"Her daughter? You're saying that Jane has a daughter?"

"Yeah, Shari, her daughter."

"Whoa, Jane, you've got it bad this time. Have you been taking your medication?"

"I am not Jane!" she insisted.

"And Shari is not your daughter."

"Of course she's not, she's Jane's! Wait, what do you mean?"

"Shari not Jane's daughter, she's Sharla's daughter."

Leeza was about to continue arguing with him when she stopped to think about it. He was making sense. That could be why Sharla took all the responsibility of caring for Shari, because she was her mother. Also, that's why Jane wasn't so eager to return to her own life, because she didn't have a daughter. She was free to live Leeza's wonderful life! She never had to come back to this complex life!

So, why did Jane tell Leeza that Shari was her daughter?

"You haven't been taking your medication, that's your problem."

"I'm not on any medication!"

"You should be. Whenever you stop taking it, you get into trouble."

"Trouble? What are you talking about?"

"Are you playing amnesia with me today?"

"No! I'm not Jane! I can't forget memories that another person has! She is living my life, in Hollywood, and I am here, living her life! But I need to get back home! Just take me to Hollywood, to my house, and we'll get this all straightened out."

"Can't do it. I have to take you back home."

"That's not my home! Can't you understand what I'm saying? I am not Jane! Look, we can get this all straightened out if you just take me to my house in Hollywood."

"Wow, Jane, if I didn't know you so well, you would really have me going. You are quite the little actress. When you get into a role, you really take on the character. But you're still you. You can't fool me. I've known you too long to fall for one of your charades."

"What can I do to convince you that I'm not Jane?"

"Absolutely nothing."

CHAPTER 24

"But I am not Jane! I am the famous Leeza Hamilton! I am a singer and performer, and I live in Hollywood and I came here – my driver, Dennis brought me here – the other night after my concert. I was walking on the beach and I met Jane there! She was wearing this cloak, and when I saw how much she looks like me, I asked her to trade places with me, just for a day! So we traded places, but she didn't come back to trade back! Well, she actually did come back the next night, but I asked her for one more day, so I could talk to her mother, and she agreed, but then the next night she didn't come back to meet me. But anyway, I AM Leeza, not Jane! You have to believe me!"

"Ahhh... well... I don't. Good story, though. I must admit, you are getting better with your stories. This is one of the best you've told me, more detailed. Good touch, the mother thing."

"I haven't ever told you a story before, because I don't know you! I've never seen you before in my life! And it's not a story! It's the truth! Just ask me any question about Leeza Hamilton's life, and I'll tell you. Come on, I'll prove it to you!"

"You could say anything you want about Leeza Hamilton and that wouldn't prove a thing – because I've never heard of her."

"What? Where have you been the last ten years? She is the most famous singer in this country, and one of the most famous performers in the whole world!"

"More delusions of grandeur, my Dear?"

"How dare you call me your Dear! I don't even know you!" Leeza was tired of acting like Plain Jane. After all, she was Leeza Hamilton, and she always got her own way!

"Don't get huffy with me, Missy. I've known you since you were knee-high to a grasshopper."

"What are you talking about? What does that mean?" She had never heard that expression before and it sounded kind of scary, since she didn't like bugs.

"Here's your house now," Sheriff Stiles said, stopping by the curb. "Let's get you inside and make sure you get your medication. I can't believe Sharla hasn't been watching you more carefully. But I guess she does have a lot on her mind, with your mom and the baby and all that."

"But I am not Jane!"

"Let's go in and talk to Sharla."

"She's probably at work."

"Not today."

"She doesn't know I'm Leeza! She thinks I'm Jane!"

"If your own sister thinks you are Jane, you are Jane. Are you telling me you are able to fool your own sister?"

"I AM fooling her! She doesn't know I'm Leeza! She thinks I am Jane!"

"That's because you ARE Jane. You have to come to grips with that. Remember who you are. Remember –" He stopped and didn't finish what he was about to say.

"I can't remember any of Jane's memories, because I am NOT Jane!"

"You can't remember because –" Again, he stopped himself.

"What are you saying? Or, what are you NOT saying? What is going on? What is the matter with Jane?"

"I'll let your sister tell you." His tone of voice changed completely. "You need to go in the house and just relax. Everything is going to be fine."

"I'm not going back in that house! Everything is NOT fine, because this is not my house!"

"You are right about that, it is Sharla's house, but this is where you live, Jane. Come on, get a grip. You have to go inside the house now."

Leeza refused to get out of the car. She was not going to stay here, now that her secret had been revealed. She wanted to go home. She needed to go home, to her own house in Hollywood, where she had been living ever since she became famous. This life of Jane's was not any kind of life she wanted to know about, much less, live.

"Come on, Jane," Sheriff Jon Stiles said soothingly. When she still didn't move, he reached in his pocket and pulled out a cell phone. He pressed a button to dial a number using speed-dial, and Leeza could hear a female voice speaking on the other end of the line.

"Yeah, I have her in the car," Sheriff Stiles said. "She doesn't know who she is, thinks she's some kind of famous person, a singer or something."

"I am!" Leeza screamed. "I'm Leeza Hamilton!"

"Did ya hear that? Yeah. Come and help me get her into the house. No, no, I don't think so. Oh, yes, that's for sure. Hmm? No, not really. She seems like she's off her medication again."

"I don't take any medication, because I'm not Jane!" Leeza shouted.

"Could ya hear that? Yeah, yeah. Okay, thanks." He closed the phone and put it back into his pocket. He turned to Leeza and said, very gently, "Your sister is coming out here and we are going to help you go in the house."

"What for? She's NOT my sister! I don't need any help! I can walk! But I'm not going back into that house! I demand that you take me home, to my own house, my real house!"

"So, this house seems kind of unreal to you?" he asked soothingly.

"No! The house is real, but it's not my house! It's not my home! I don't live here!"

Sharla approached the police car. Leeza locked the door so she couldn't open it.

"Come on, Jane, we don't have time for games today," she said.

Leeza looked straight ahead, avoiding looking at Sharla.

"So who do you think you are this time?" Sharla asked through the closed window.

"Jane, let us help you," Sheriff Stiles said. "I don't want to have to call Doc Munsinger."

"Who is Doc Munsinger?" Leeza asked.

Sheriff Stiles got out of the car and said something to Sharla that Leeza couldn't hear. Sharla went back into the house and the sheriff returned to his seat in the car

"Great! You're taking me home!" Leeza said.

The sheriff didn't respond, nor did he start the car.

"Well, let's go!" Leeza said.

Sheriff Stiles looked at her with a look of pity on his face. After a minute or two, Sharla came out of the house and walked over to the driver's side of the police car. Sheriff Stiles got out of the car and Sharla sat in his seat while he walked around to the back of the car.

"What happened?" Sharla asked.

"Nothing," Leeza said. "I'm just not who you think I am."

"Who do I think you are?"

"Your sister, Jane."

"You are correct. You ARE my sister, Jane, and I do think you are. As a matter of fact, I know you are."

"No, I'm not your sister! I'm Leeza Hamilton!"

"I'm sure you are," Sharla said, nodding her head.

"I just want to go home, back to my house, my own house, in Hollywood."

"That sounds just lovely," Sharla said. She reached around Leeza and before she knew what was happening, Leeza realized Sharla had stuck her with a needle.

The effect of the drug was immediate. Leeza's head felt heavy, her thinking dulled. She was inside a cocoon, a fluffy, puffy, soft cocoon, and the sounds of the outside world became muffled. She was going to hibernate and emerge as a butterfly. She thought she might be giggling, but the giggles may have only been on the inside, because she couldn't feel her lips. She couldn't feel anything. Sharla's voice made some strange, distant, underwater sounds and Leeza was moving through the air, toward the house. Her mind had a reason for her not to go into the house, but her body was propelled, not of its own accord, to the front door. The instant she saw the couch in the living room, her body folded onto it. She didn't feel it. She closed her eyes for a moment.

CHAPTER 25

Leeza opened her eyes and she was at home, in her own room! A few things were out of place, but she was at home, at her own house in Hollywood! She stood up from her couch and she slowly explored her room, her dresser, her desk, her nightstands, her king-sized bed, her chairs, her enormous walk-in closet. There was not a red item in this world, and she was comforted by that realization. She was home again!

The first thing she wanted to do was to get in her hot tub. She had gone too many days without a massage or a dip in the hot tub, and her muscles were aching. She walked through her enormous walk-through closet, examining her beautiful selection of clothes, all neatly hanging or folded by one of her staff, and up the stairs to her tub room, where she had a large hot tub. She tested the water in the hot tub – it was perfect! They always kept it full for her, so she could get in it whenever she wanted, and it was always set at the temperature she loved. She slipped out of her clothes and eased herself into the water. Yes, this was exactly what she needed.

One thing she loved about this room was that it had windows all around it. It was a circular room above the third floor, so she could look out the windows at her grounds, but no one could see her from down there. She gazed out the window, relaxing in the pleasure of being home. Ahh, this was the life; no, this was *her* life! She had had enough of a taste of a so-called meaningful life – now she could see that her own life had tons of meaning.

As she watched out the window, she saw Karman run across the grass to meet her boyfriend. Everyone knew she was dating the gardener – what was his name? He had a cool name, Leeza thought... what was it? Oh, yes, oh, yes, Dodge Dishman. He was really quite good-looking. Karman ran to the hedges where he had been trimming them, and she threw her arms around him. He swung her around in a circle while they kissed. They spoke for a minute, then, hand-in-hand, they walked to the edge of the property and went into the gardener's shed. Leeza felt good, as if she were being included in their romantic moment. After all, she reasoned, they wouldn't have met if they didn't both work for her. She understood how important she was to both of them, financially and personally.

Leeza put the small of her back against the jets in the tub for a few minutes. Then she let another jet massage her shoulders and neck. She was feeling so relaxed, she felt like she could just fall asleep in the tub. After a few more minutes, she was refreshed and ready to eat something, a nice meal specially prepared for her by Hans. Hans was a wonderful chef, a terrific meal planner, and a person genuinely concerned about her health. She could attribute her all-around well being to his love for making her great meals.

She climbed out of the hot tub and wrapped herself in one of her luxurious, thick, soft towels. She inhaled the fresh scent of lavender – when they did her laundry, they always used a lavender rinse on her clothes and towels. She went into her closet, trying to decide which of her cozy outfits to wear. Inspired by the smell of lavender, she chose a soft purple top and a pair of designer cut-offs.

She called for Nita. Nita always came when she called. She stayed in the room just down the steps from Leeza's, taking care of things for Leeza and waiting for Leeza to call for her services. Leeza loved Nita – she was her favorite assistant, always so cheerful, so prompt, so responsive, and also so understanding. Nita would be the one who would be most sympathetic to Leeza's adventure – or misadventure – at Jane's house, living Jane's life. Nita would also be the most likely to have suspected that Jane wasn't Leeza.

The events of the past few days were so out of touch with Leeza's real life, she began to wonder if she had just dreamed it all, the whole thing: Jane and Sharla and Shari and the beach and the house and the sheriff and everything. She could have dreamed it – she had a great imagination, and she often had extremely detailed dreams of events that spanned days and nights. Oh, it didn't matter now: she was home again!

She wondered what time it was. Nita would tell her. Leeza didn't have any use for clocks in her room – they were so demanding, always forcing a person to do something at a particular moment. Leeza let others watch the clock and keep track of time for her – she had much more important business that required her attention. Where was Nita, anyway?

"Nita!" she shouted. "Where are you?"

CHAPTER 26

The door opened and Nita came bouncing into Leeza's room. She was like that, always bouncing from place to place, with a smile on her face. Leeza appreciated her energy as well as her positive attitude. It was so good to be home!

"Hey, Girl! What do you need?" Nita asked, fluffing pillows and straightening the bed covers.

"Oh, man, I've really missed you!" Leeza said with a sigh.

"You've only been asleep for a couple of hours," Nita replied. "You know, those new stage outfits you ordered have arrived and it would be nice if you could try them on today, see if I need to take them in or anything, or if we need to send any back. You know how those things often look great in the picture, then when you get them, they look like a bunch of rags sewn together."

"Stage outfits?" Leeza really had been gone a long time. She didn't remember ordering any new stage outfits.

"You hungry? Hans has your lunch all ready for you. He just got a load of fresh avocados, and he has made the most scrumptious creation I have ever seen." Nita began straightening the items on the dressing table.

"You've ever seen? Don't you mean tasted?"

"Oh, Girl, you know what I mean." Nita liked to eat. She enjoyed eating and she wasn't ashamed of asking for seconds. She was a great encouragement to Hans. If he were only cooking for Leeza, he would either have to buy a very small amount of food, or throw out a large amount. Leeza didn't ever eat much, but Hans fed Leeza's entire staff, which was really like family to her.

"The answer is yes! I am hungry! Let's go downstairs now!" Leeza said excitedly. These past few days she had missed too many of those great meals Hans loved to cook.

A thought occurred to her... had Nita noticed a difference, with Jane here instead of her?

"Nita," Leeza said, grabbing her arm, "do I seem different to you?"

"Girl, you are the most different person I know. Every moment you are transforming into a new personality, which is why I still think you should change your name to Leeza Chameleon."

"No, I mean, did you notice anything strange about me yesterday? Or the day before?"

"You know I was off yesterday. Remember? I went to see my sister – oh, you have to see her baby! She is soooo cute! I just love those little hands, the tiny fingers, and, you know, each one has a miniature fingernail on it! She is a doll! And that hair! I would never believe a tiny baby could have so much hair! She was over nine pounds when she was born, and, true to the family, she is growing every day! Can you believe she is already more than sixteen pounds? She has already outgrown her baby clothes and she's not even a month old yet! I got her the cutest little outfit, like a cheerleader outfit, and she looks just about like a little teddy bear in it, with those chubby little legs, and her little arms just sticking out, hands all over the place. I didn't know babies that young could suck their thumbs, but she's constantly trying to find hers and stick it in her mouth. Oh, she's the cutest! I'll bring her over sometime so you can see her. You are just going to love her!"

"What's her name?" Leeza asked, picturing baby Shari in her mind.

"She named her Shari Marie," Nita said, "Shari, after our aunt, and Marie after our grandmother. She says God gave her that name, and it suits her. She looks exactly like a Shari Marie. She couldn't have any other name! Oh, she is SO cute!"

"Shari?" Leeza asked.

"Yeah, isn't it beautiful? I tell you, she is, without question, the most beautiful baby in the world. You have got to see her."

"Sure, bring her over, anytime," Leeza said thoughtfully. She had never in her life known anyone named Shari, and now, just this week, she knew two babies with that name. That had to be a most unlikely coincidence.

"Come on, Hans has everything waiting for us." Nita took Leeza by the hand to start her moving towards the door.

"Yeah, I'm starving!" Leeza said. She really couldn't remember the last time she had eaten.

Before they could leave the room, Karman breezed in without knocking.

"Oh, I didn't realize you were back!" she said. "I'm so sorry! Excuse me for not knocking!"

"Hey, it's okay," Leeza said, as Nita gave Karman a stern look. "So how are you doing today?"

Karman blushed. "I am really having a good day, thank you for asking," she said. "Hey, are you feeling better today? I mean, no more of that crazy talk? You really look a lot better. You look like yourself again."

"Of course she's herself, Girl!" Nita said. "Who else would she be?"

"I feel wonderful!" Leeza said, surprising both of them. She knew they expected her to snap orders at them or remind them of some overlooked duties, but today she was just happy to be with them. They were her friends; really, they were more than just members of her staff. Leeza was just noticing that they each had lives of their own; not everything they did revolved around serving her. They weren't servants. They were more like family to her, she told herself. She couldn't bring herself to tell them that, though. They would have to figure it out, the same way she had.

"We're going downstairs to eat," Leeza told Karman. "Come on. Have you eaten? Come and sit with us. We have a lot of catching up to do."

"We do?" Nita and Karman said together. They looked at each other. The three of them burst out laughing. They all held hands to go to lunch.

As they left her room and entered the hallway, Leeza suddenly stopped, pulling Nita and Karman to a stop also. Leeza stared at the walls.

"What's the matter?" Nita asked. She looked at Leeza. "Are you okay? Is something the matter? What's wrong?"

"When did this happen?" Leeza asked, horrified.

"When did what happen?" Nita asked, looking around the hallway.

"This! All this! Who did this?" Leeza demanded.

"Who did what?" Karman asked.

"This red paint! Why are these splotches of red paint all over my walls? And on the carpet! My beautiful white carpet is ruined!" Leeza fell to her knees and began to examine the bright red paint stains that were all over the carpet.

"What are you talking about?" Nita asked.

"What do you mean? Red! Can't you see all this red?" Leeza looked around frantically, extremely disturbed by this red invasion of her house.

"Red? I don't see anything red in this hallway, or in this entire house, for that matter. Everyone in this house knows that red is forbidden in this house," Karman said.

"Girl, there is nothing red anywhere around here," Nita agreed.

"Are you blind? Or color blind? There is red paint all over the place! Get someone up here to repaint these walls! And call someone to replace the carpet! This is horrendous! No red is allowed in here!" Leeza wondered what was wrong with them, with their eyes.

"Calm down, calm down! You don't want to get yourself in a panic. Maybe you are seeing a reflection or something." Nita said soothingly.

"I am not in a panic! And it's not a reflection! Don't you look at me like I'm crazy! I am not crazy!" Leeza insisted.

"You are eccentric, that's for sure, but I would never say you are crazy," Nita said, stroking Leeza's hair, in an effort to calm her.

"Then get this cleaned up!" Leeza shouted.

"I'll get someone up here right away, before I eat lunch," Nita promised. "Come on, let's go to the dining room. Everything is ready for you there."

"I can't stand the sight of it," Leeza said, closing her eyes. "Lead me, if you please. I can't look at it." She reached out for Nita's hand.

"Whatever you want," Nita said, taking her hand.

Leeza kept her eyes tightly closed as she let Nita lead her down the hallway to the stairs. The hallway seemed a lot longer than usual while she had her eyes closed. They kept walking and walking, but they didn't get to the steps. What was going on? She was really getting hungry! They walked and walked and walked and walked. She was afraid to open her eyes, but she didn't remember the hallway being this long. Maybe they were taking very small steps, but even so, shouldn't they be there by now?

"Are we there yet?" she asked.

CHAPTER 27

"Are we where yet?" an unfamiliar voice answered.

Leeza stopped walking and struggled to open her eyes. She suddenly felt as if she were coming out of a deep, deep sleep. Her eyes didn't want to open; they wanted to just stay closed. What was happening to her? She needed to open her eyes so she could walk down the steps, so she could go and eat, but her eyes refused to open. She moved her mouth to ask Nita for help, but she could make no sound. Her mouth seemed to be full of cotton. Her eyelids were so heavy, there was no way she could move them out of her way so she could see. Her muscles were so relaxed, she had to go back to sleep. Her energy was drained and her ambition to get to the table was gone. Her hunger would wait until later, when she was awake enough to want to eat.

Some time later, she had no idea how long, she opened her eyes. The red was gone from the walls, but the walls were also gone; at least her walls were gone. She was in a familiar place, but where was she? She couldn't hear anything except the sound of the jets flying overhead, flying so closely, they were roaring in her ears. The room was strangely dim – was it night already? No, it didn't seem to be dark; the room was just dim because of the lack of lighting and the dark walls, the natural wood walls. She must be dreaming, because she didn't know where she was... or did she?

She was at Sharla's house again! She was in the office. How did she get back here? She needed to get away from here immediately! She tried to sit, but she couldn't move. At first she thought she might be paralyzed, then she realized that something was restraining her. She was tied down, on some kind of hospital bed! She remembered, a long time ago, Sharla and the sheriff were trying to convince her to come into the house, but she had refused. Now she was in the house. What were they doing to her? She made an attempt to call to Sharla, but her voice was gone. Her mouth felt so funny. She really needed some water.

The roar of the jets continued, but another sound came into her range of hearing, a moaning or a crying or... people were talking in low voices and she couldn't understand what they were saying. She couldn't see anyone in the room, but then, from this position, she could only see a small portion of the room. She had to get out of here!

Sharla's face came into her line of vision. Her face looked so large, so obtuse, so unusual, as she stared at Leeza, her big face changing shape as it grew closer and closer to Leeza's face. She didn't say anything. Then the sheriff stuck his big head right beside Sharla's enormous head as she examined Leeza's face. They moved their mouths at each other, but they didn't speak to Leeza. Leeza wanted to say something, but her mouth refused to cooperate with her central command system in her brain. What was happening to her?

Leeza drifted in and out of consciousness for moments or days, she wasn't sure which. She knew she was very hungry, but she couldn't stay awake long enough to eat, or to even tell them that she wanted to eat. She would be in the room for a moment, then she would be in blackness, then back in the room, then back in the blackness again. She did not like this feeling at all, this loss of control, this loss of awareness of time and space... but right now she was just too tired to do anything about it. She let herself slip back into that world of nothingness, wrapped in a giant cushioned envelope.

When she opened her eyes again, the day was bright and the sun was shining in the room. She felt refreshed, recharged and ready to face the day. What day was it? How long had she been here? Where was she?

She discovered she was no longer a prisoner in the office at Sharla's house, but she now she was in Jane's bed, wrapped in the covers. The whole area had been cleaned – no clothes were strewn around the room, everything was in perfect order, and she could smell that even the bedding had been washed. She started to sit, but was unable – not because she was tied to the bed, but because her muscles were so weak.

A sudden thought caused her to panic: did she miss her concert? She had to know what day it was! She had to get back to her own life so she could perform! Many people were depending on her – not only her staff and the crew, but her thousands of fans, her loyal and loving fans, would be extremely disappointed if she didn't show for her concert. How could she perform if she couldn't move?

She struggled, using all of her will power as well as all of her strength, to pull herself into a sitting position. She threw the heavy covers off her and forced her legs to hang over the edge of the bed. She stopped to get her breath. How long had it been since she had eaten? How long had she been here, not moving? Her muscles were telling her they had not been used for quite some time. She had to move them. She had to bring herself back to life, to her own life, not the life of an invalid!

She began by wiggling her toes. She looked at them, thought about moving them, sent the signal to them, and they began to move. Once both feet had moving toes, she began moving her ankles, rotating her feet, making little circles, to the left and then to the right. She enlarged the circles, happy with the way her body was responding to her brain. She dangled her feet, swinging her legs. She needed to stand on these legs, to walk on these legs, to dance with these legs.

She stopped to rest for a few minutes, feeling her heart pound. She knew now that Sharla must have drugged her, thinking she was Jane, who obviously was taking some kind of medication for a mental problem. Everything was so logical to Leeza now. Jane had to be watched, and she was unable to care for herself. When the sheriff had given Leeza a ride, he really thought she was Jane, and since Leeza had been insisting that she was not Jane, they must have assumed she had some sort of breakdown, so they thought they could take care of it by giving her some medication.

Leeza wiggled her hands and fingers. Her skin felt so dry. She really missed all the special kinds of lotion that were at her house. Every day, she loved to pamper herself by selecting just the right hand lotion, the scent depending on her mood and the weather, and then rubbing it into her hands, between her fingers, up her arms, until it was all absorbed by her skin. For the rest of the day, she would enjoy drifts of that scent when she put her hands near her face, even after washing her hands. The only bottle of lotion Plain Jane had in her room was unscented. What was the use of that? It was merely functional, not enjoyable.

She raised her arms above her head in an attempt to stretch. Oh, ow, her muscles were so weak and so sore. This was not a familiar feeling to Leeza. She was strong, always moving, constantly exercising or stretching or dancing, pushing her muscles to their limits. She had to get herself out of this condition. She knew she couldn't do it alone, but she couldn't trust Sharla – or Jane. She didn't have anyone else in the world who knew where she was. There was no one here who could help her... or was there?

CHAPTER 28

She bowed her head and she began to pray. She believed in God, and He was everywhere. She knew He was the One who had blessed her with what it took for her to become famous. She knew everything she had came from Him.

"Dear Father in heaven," she said softly, "I know I have ignored You for a long time and I ask for You to forgive me for that. I know You are here with me now. I know You can hear me now. Please help me now?"

She believed that He had heard her, and He gave her the strength to stand on her feet. She stood still for a moment, and then she stretched her arms to the left and to the right, reaching as high as she could, and then bending to touch the floor. She could walk. He gave her the strength to walk around the room. She let the sunlight shine on her, giving her some solar power as she absorbed its warmth. She looked down upon the nightgown she was wearing – did people actually wear these? – and pulled it over her head. She went to Jane's closet and selected some more appropriate clothes. She dressed to leave the house and to leave this town.

She stopped what she was doing. Thinking about God triggered a memory in her mind. She remembered a Sunday School lesson from long ago, when, as a girl, she had attended Sunday School. It was about ten lepers who asked Jesus to heal them. He gave them instructions and when they obeyed Him, they were healed. Only one of the lepers came back to thank Him. He asked that one, "Were there not ten healed? Where are the other nine?" The lesson Leeza had gotten from that story was to always say 'thank you' when God did something she asked. Right now, she paused and thanked Him for giving her strength. Then she was able to continue with her mission, to get ready to get out of here.

Leeza wanted to put on her makeup the way she usually wore it, but she couldn't find any makeup in Jane's bathroom. She realized that the house was quite still – she couldn't hear any baby noises or any type of sound at all. She clapped her hands together, just to be sure she hadn't lost her hearing – nope, she heard that clap. Just to be safe, she went very quietly to Sharla's bathroom. Leeza knew she had makeup, because she was always wearing it. Leeza wasn't as proficient at applying her own makeup as Karman and Nita were – one of them always did it for her – but she knew how she liked her face to look, and her look was not plain. She had never been accused of looking 'natural,' yet her makeup was applied to accent her features, the way it was intended to do.

She looked in Sharla's mirror and made up her face so she looked the way she usually looked during the daytime. On stage, it was a different story, she wore much more makeup, because everything had to be magnified; but during the day, she looked like this. She smiled to see herself looking like herself, the famous Leeza Hamilton, again. Now, she had to do something with her hair. What would Karman do? She would just take a comb or brush and whip Leeza's hair into style. No, she sprayed something on it; but did she spray before or after styling? Leeza made a commitment at that moment to start paying more attention to details, acknowledging that if she knew her own phone number or address, she would not be in this mess today.

Leeza combed and brushed and wetted and stretched and twisted her hair until finally, she looked more like herself than she looked like Jane. Now nobody could mistake her for Plain Jane, because she was anything but plain. She put everything away in its proper place, another first for her, and went down to the kitchen. She needed to eat.

What would Hans do? He would whip up something fantastic in a hurry, just using items he had on hand in the kitchen. Of course, he had a large pantry, a huge refrigerator and three freezers, along with an almost unlimited food budget, so he had quite few more choices than Leeza had right now. She looked in this little, run-down refrigerator and decided on a ham and cheese sandwich, on white bread, which was her only choice. She could also choose either to use mayonnaise or not use mayonnaise, because that was the only condiment they had on the refrigerator door. The cheese didn't look like it was real cheese, and the ham looked like some kind of pressed meat, but she was so hungry, she had to eat it anyway. Sharla had been letting her starve, almost to death!

Leeza made the sandwich and ate it quickly. She was so hungry, she felt as if she could eat another – but she didn't. Instead, she selected a nice, firm, juicy red apple and quickly ate it as well. She washed it down with a glass of whole milk, something she hadn't tasted since she had left home. She loved milk, but she didn't love milk fat. However, again, she didn't have a choice. She refused to drink soda pop, and right now she needed more than water.

When she was finished eating, she washed the utensils she had used and cleaned the counters and tabletop. The kitchen looked as if no one had even been in here. Strengthened by the food she had eaten, Leeza boldly went out the front door, to the outside world. She inhaled deeply – this fresh air was really something to savor! With the fresh air bringing new oxygen to her brain, she also received a plan.

Sharla was not home, and neither was Shari, so that meant Sharla must be at work, and Shari at the babysitter's. Leeza wanted more than anything to just go back to her own life, but she had no way to get there. She had to go about this a different way. She had to find out more about Jane, so she could know what to expect, and how she should not behave. She had to disclose her true self to the people of this town, so they would know who she really was. Somebody would surely help her get home, and, in the process, help Jane get to where she could get the medical attention she needed.

Only one person could help Leeza discover who Jane really was, and what was the matter with her. She bravely walked with her head exposed, revealing to this town the famous Leeza Hamilton.

CHAPTER 29

She walked up the sidewalk to the house where Jane's mother lived and knocked on the door. The same lady answered as did when she came here with Sharla.

"What can I do for you?" the lady asked coldly.

"I'm here to see Ruby," Leeza said.

"She can't see anyone right now." She began to close the door.

"Wait!" Leeza said, grabbing the door. "I really need to see her."

"You watch yourself, young lady," she said, holding the door.

"Please! I won't be long. I just need to see her for a minute or two."

"I won't have you upsetting her! She has been having a good day today."

"That's great! That's wonderful! I want her to continue to have a good day!"

"Then she shouldn't be seeing you."

"I'm not who you think I am!" Leeza said. "Look at me. I'm not Jane. I'm... I'm a friend of hers."

The lady stopped and took a good look at Leeza. "Is this another one of your tricks? I've heard about you."

"No, I just look sort of like Jane, but I'm not Jane." How could she convince this lady of who she really was? "I'm Leeza Hamilton, I live in Hollywood, and you might have seen me on TV," she said.

The lady continued to look at her.

"So, what's your name? We haven't met."

"You know who I am," she said sternly.

"I don't know, because I'm not Jane."

"Did you take your medication?"

"I'm not Jane! I don't take medication! I'm Leeza Hamilton!"

"Why do you want to see Ruby, Leeza Hamilton?"

"I just want to talk to her for a few minutes. I promise I won't upset her. I promise. Scout's honor." Leeza had been a Girl Scout, long ago.

"You were a Boy Scout?" the lady asked.

"I was a Girl Scout," Leeza corrected.

"What's the Girl Scout creed?"

"They don't have one."

"Yes, they do." The lady set her lips firmly.

"Okay, they have the Girl Scout Promise, but it's not called a creed."

"What is it?"

"Oh, you know!

> 'On my honor,
> I will try
> To do my duty,
> To God and my country,
> To help other people every day,
> Especially those at home.' " Leeza recited.

"That's the Girl Scout Promise? Did you make that up?"

"Oh, no! That's not right! That's the Brownie Promise! This is the Girl Scout Promise:

> 'On my honor,
> I will try
> To do my duty,
> To God and my country,
> To help other people at all times,
> And to obey the Girl Scout Law.' "

"So, what's the Girl Scout Law?" the lady asked suspiciously.

Leeza had to think for a few seconds.

> " 'I will do my best to be
> Honest and fair,
> Friendly and helpful,
> Considerate and caring,
> Courageous and strong, and
> Responsible for what I say and do...'

...and I can't remember the rest."

"Wow! You really were a Girl Scout! Well, from one Girl Scout to another, I have to trust you. Come on in. But please, don't tire her. And if she starts to get upset..." She opened the door and let Leeza enter.

"I won't let her get upset. I just want to do my Girl Scout duty, to be considerate and caring, and you can be sure I will be responsible for what I say and do."

"By the way, my name is Sylvia, and I have been taking care of your mother – Jane's mother – ever since she got out of the hospital. The last time, I mean. She came to live with me after the last time in the hospital."

"Why was she in the hospital?"

"The breakdown. Didn't you know?"

"Breakdown?"

"Yeah, she had problems before that, but then when she had the breakdown, well, after that, she couldn't live at home any more. Sharla couldn't even take care of her. And even after all this time, she hasn't improved in any way. As a matter of fact, she has gotten worse."

"Is she on medication?" Leeza asked.

"Of course! She can't function without her medication. You should know that. Oh, that's right, you aren't Jane now, are you?"

"I have never been Jane!"

"Relax, don't get all in a huff. Let's go see if Ruby's awake now. If she's asleep, I'm afraid I can't allow you to disturb her."

"Fair enough."

Leeza followed Sylvia to Ruby's room where Sylvia tapped lightly on the door. Ruby didn't answer. Sylvia eased open the door and peeked into the room.

"It's okay," she said quietly to Leeza. "She's awake. Ruby, you have some company. Ruby? Can you hear me?"

Ruby didn't respond. Just as the last time Leeza came to visit, she was sitting in a wheelchair, looking out the window.

"Can she walk?" Leeza whispered to Sylvia. Sylvia shook her head.

"How are you doing today, Ruby?" Leeza asked, recalling that she herself still didn't know what day it was.

Ruby continued to stare out the window.

"Ruby," Leeza said, "I just came to sit with you for a few minutes. Would you like me to rub your feet?"

Ruby seemed to come into the room.

"My feet?" she asked, her expression beginning to show some sort of understanding.

"Yes, I would like to rub your feet, if you don't mind. Sylvia, do you have any lotion I can use?"

"I'll go get some. You just stay here with Ruby. Ruby loves carnations, don't you, Ruby? And I just got some lotion that smells like carnations." Sylvia left Leeza alone with Ruby. Leeza removed one of Ruby's slipper-socks and began to stroke her foot, gently.

"Ruby, I need to ask you something," Leeza said, hoping that Ruby would stay with her for a few minutes. Ruby tilted her head so she was looking at Leeza.

"Ruby, what is the matter with Jane?" she asked. "Your daughter, Jane. What's the matter with her?"

"You are not my daughter."

"No, I am not your daughter. My name is Leeza. Jane and I look kind of alike, but I'm not Jane. I'm Leeza."

"You are not my daughter," she repeated.

"You're right, I'm not."

"Jane is not my daughter."

"Jane isn't your daughter? I thought Jane and Sharla were both your daughters."

"Sharla is a good girl," Ruby said. "She comes to see me. She takes care of me. She would never hurt me."

"No, she wouldn't. And neither would Jane. Jane doesn't want to hurt you either."

"Jane is not my daughter!" she shouted.

"My goodness! What is going on in here?" Sylvia asked, returning with a bottle of lotion in her hand. She gave the bottle to Leeza.

"Jane is not my daughter!" Ruby repeated, not quite so loudly.

"Don't get yourself all upset, Ruby, dear," Sylvia said. "I'll go get your medication."

"Does she have to take it now?" Leeza asked.

"It keeps her calm."

"Why does she have to always be calm? It's not natural to always be calm." Leeza looked at Sylvia.

"You don't know her. You haven't been here. She can really get upset."

"Everyone gets upset sometimes!"

"Well, we like to keep her calm."

"With drugs? Like they keep Jane calm?"

"Do you want me to call your sister?" Sylvia asked calmly, as she moved toward the door.

"I don't have a sister!"

"I think you need to go home now, and you need to take your medication."

"You can't just give everyone some medication to keep them calm all the time!"

"Now, now, just relax," Sylvia said, in that awful, relaxing tone.

Leeza held her tongue while she rubbed lotion in her hands to warm it, before letting it touch Ruby's foot. Since Sylvia doubted her words, that she was not Jane, Leeza would have to convince her by her actions. She simply would not act in any way like Jane. She would be composed and in control, every moment. Sylvia kept a close watch on her as she applied the lotion to Ruby's foot.

"A good girl would never kill her father," Ruby said.

Leeza stopped rubbing her foot and looked straight at Ruby.

"What did you say?"

"She's talking crazy. I'll get her medication." Sylvia made a move to leave the room, then she decided to stay. Leeza knew she felt like she had to keep an eye on her, to monitor their conversation.

"Ruby, what did you mean by that?" Leeza asked.

"She didn't know what she meant," Sylvia insisted.

"Ruby?" Leeza said.

"I think you better leave now," Sylvia said.

"No!" Ruby shouted, stunning both Leeza and Sylvia.

"I think I better stay a little longer," Leeza said. She resumed the foot massage. Sylvia didn't move.

"Ruby? How's that?" Leeza asked. "Does your foot feel better?"

"My foot," Ruby said. She smiled.

"Yeah, doesn't that feel great?" Leeza asked. She was making contact with Ruby, two-way contact.

"Sharla is a good girl," Ruby said again, nodding her head.

"Yes, she is," Sylvia agreed. "She comes and visits you every day. She is a good daughter. You are very blessed to have her for a daughter."

"Bless you," Ruby said, looking straight at Leeza. She gave her a sincere smile.

"Thank you," Leeza said, returning her smile. They looked at each other for a few minutes in silence.

"You are not my daughter," Ruby said.

"You're right," Leeza said. "I am not your daughter." She continued smiling and rubbing Ruby's feet.

"You ruined everything," Ruby finally said.

"What? What do you mean?" Leeza asked. "What are you talking about?"

"You better go now," Sylvia said to Leeza.

"I'm not leaving until I finish both feet!" Leeza said.

"Both feet," Ruby said, bobbing her head.

"Ruby, this IS your daughter!" Sylvia shouted. "She is the one who did this to you!" she cried.

"No, I didn't do anything!" Leeza insisted. "I just came here to help you!"

"Help me?" Ruby shrieked. "Help me? You destroyed our lives! Why did you have to kill him?"

A vision of those awful blood spatters flashed before Leeza's eyes. She closed her eyes until the red disappeared. Sylvia ran out of the room.

"I didn't kill anyone!" Leeza cried. More red blood splotches flashed in her field of vision. She blinked several times so she could focus on here and now.

"You couldn't just let it go! You couldn't just leave it alone! You had to ruin everything!" Ruby cried, moving her arms wildly.

"Do you think I'm Jane? I'm not Jane! I am NOT Jane!"

"He wasn't going to hurt her! Why couldn't you just mind your own business? Why couldn't you just stay out of it, and leave well enough alone?"

"Hurt her? Hurt who? What are you talking about? Ruby, what do you mean?"

"Everything was just fine, before you had to barge in and ruin it," Ruby said, sobbing.

"Now, now, Ruby, everything is fine," Sylvia said, as she scurried into the room. Before Leeza could comprehend what she was doing, she stuck a needle in Ruby's arm. Ruby's eyes immediately glazed over.

"Why did you do that?" Leeza demanded, trying to see if any trace of Ruby was still with them.

"I had to," Sylvia said. "Did you see how upset she was getting?"

"Upset? Do you want to see upset?" Leeza cried. "She was just talking to me! She was starting to tell me something!"

"As if you didn't know! Why are you trying to hurt her, by making her relive it again? You already put her through enough! You just leave her alone! I want you to get out of here, and never come back!"

"What was she talking about? What was she trying to tell me?"

"Just get out! And don't come back!" Sylvia pointed towards the door, as if that would make Leeza leave.

"I'm not leaving until you tell me what she was talking about! What did Jane do? Tell me!" Leeza stood with her arms crossed.

"You get out of here, right this minute!"

"Did Jane kill her father?"

"I am calling Sheriff Stiles right now," Sylvia said, reaching for the phone.

"No!" Leeza shouted, not wanting another incident with him. She had to get away from him, not bring him to her. He would just send her back to Sharla's house again, to be drugged again. "I'm leaving! You don't need to call him."

Sylvia escorted Leeza to the front door. After she shut it behind her, Leeza heard the lock click. Her heart was pounding, as if it were about to burst out of her chest. With each heartbeat, she could see blotches of blood. She was positive that the movie she had seen, the one about the girl killing her father, and the newspaper article she had found in the office at Sharla's house were both about Jane. Jane must have killed her father, and somehow, that had driven their mother crazy. Leeza had to get out of this town immediately; yet she couldn't risk being seen, as Leeza or Jane.

CHAPTER 30

To avoid detection, she rushed back towards Sharla's house and cut through the yard, down the stairway to the beach. Although she wasn't wearing the red cloak, neither did she look like Plain Jane. She had chosen Jane's most outrageous outfit, and with her Leeza-style makeup and hair, she couldn't possibly be mistaken for Jane. She slipped off her shoes so she could run on the beach. She went down to the edge of the water, where the sand was firm, and began to run south as fast as she could, which wasn't very fast, since her muscles hadn't been used in a few days. She pushed herself to the limit, running, running, away from the house, away from the town. She felt as if she could run all the way to the beach at Santa Monica, and then she would be able to get back home. She knew her way home from there; besides, she would be able to blend in with the thousands of people who were always populating that beach.

She ran as far as she could, then she walked for a few minutes to catch her breath. Then she started running again. It felt so good to run! She felt so free! She ran and ran, gaining energy with each step, as she got further away from that awful, confining town. She slowed to a jog for a few minutes, and then she stopped, trapped. The shoreline ahead jutted out into the ocean – this beach didn't go any farther. She had three choices: she could swim around the huge rock; she could climb up the hill and go over it; or she could hike up the beach and go up near the road. She knew the road was near, because, although she could not see the passing cars, she could hear them.

Swimming would be too dangerous, she noted, as she watched the waves crashing into the giant rock that was blocking her path. That choice was not a choice. Climbing the rock could be very dangerous. She could not see a clear path, and, from down here, this side looked quite steep. The only logical way she could choose would be to go up near the road.

Maybe she could stay away from the road. She could walk beside it and not be seen. Maybe she was far enough away from the town so that they wouldn't be looking for her here. Either way, she had to take the risk, just until she got past this giant rock and could return to the safety of the beach.

The beach was wide at this point, so the walk to the road was long. As soon as she got to the edge of the sand, to the rocky area, she stopped and pulled on her shoes. She had to go slowly at this point, because of the rocks, then she came to an area of tall grass. She looked for a path, and not seeing one, she forged her own path. The final stretch was very steep, and she had to climb hand-over-hand to pull herself up to the top level, also filled with tall grass. As she finally got to the edge of the grass, she stopped short. She was in a parking lot, and Sharla was standing by a car, waiting for her.

"You had me so worried!" she said to Leeza. "Why did you go running off like that? Sylvia called me and said you went to her house and freaked out! And you upset Mom! What's the matter?"

CHAPTER 31

"I am not Jane," Leeza confessed, defeated. How could Jane's own sister not recognize that she, Leeza Hamilton, was not Jane?

"If you're not Jane, who are you, then?" Sharla asked. She truly seemed concerned. Was this a trap?

"I am Leeza Hamilton," she said, staying away from the car.

"Leeza Hamilton?"

"Yes, the singer. You must have heard of me. Everyone has heard of me."

"I see," Sharla said, nodding. "How did you get here? Why were you pretending to be Jane?"

"My driver brought me up here a few nights ago. I met Jane on the beach. When she pointed out that we looked just alike, we decided to switch places. I needed a break from my hectic life."

"You needed a break?" Sharla eyed her suspiciously.

"Yeah, I just finished a concert, and I was really feeling like I needed... well, something more."

"Something more? Doesn't Leeza Hamilton have just about everything?"

"Things, yeah, but there's more to life than just things."

"Yes, I agree," Sharla said. "There is much more to life than just things."

"Jane was supposed to meet me on the beach again, so we could trade back, but she didn't show up. I need to get back to Hollywood so I can get ready for my next concert. What day is it, anyway? Thanks to the tranquilizers you gave me, I kind of lost track of time, but I really need to get home." Leeza looked around for anyone else who could help her.

"Do you ever know what day it is?"

"I don't usually have to bother myself with details, because my staff takes care of all that so I can focus on what I need to do."

"You have it all figured out, don't you?" Sharla nodded.

"What are you talking about?"

"You have the perfect escape." Sharla pierced her with her stare. Leeza looked away from her, away from those accusing eyes.

"Perfect, it's not, but the only escape I want to make is from this town, so I can get back home, to my own house in Hollywood."

"I can take you home." She stepped closer to Leeza.

"No, thanks, I have already been there. Your friend, Sheriff Jon Stiles, promised me the same thing, and he took me back to your house." Leeza took a step backwards, away from Sharla.

"I'll drive you to Hollywood, to your own house."

"Yeah, right. I'm not falling for that again." Leeza shook her head.

"No, really, I'll take you to your house. Isn't that where you said Jane is?"

"I was hoping my driver would bring her back here, so we could change places again, but I guess she loves my life so much, she decided to stay there a little longer than we planned. I can't just keep waiting for her to come back here. I need to get back there."

"So, if I drive you to your house, you and Jane can trade places there. You can stay there and I'll bring her back here. How does that sound?"

"It sounds good, but, to be honest, I don't really trust you."

"Before, I thought you were Jane. Now I know who you really are."

"Really? You really believe me?" Leeza was encouraged.

"Well, to be honest, I was wondering what was the matter with my sister these past few days. She didn't seem to be herself. Now I know why. You are not her. That explains a lot of things."

"So... you believe me."

"Yes, I believe you."

"You promise?" Leeza looked into Sharla's face to see if she were telling the truth.

"Of course!"

"Before I get in the car with you, tell me what happened to Jane. What did she do? Why is she so weird? Why did your mom say all those things about her?"

"Oh, you don't want to know."

"Yes, I do."

"It's a long story."

"I have time. Seems like all I have is time, until I can get out of this place and get back to my own life."

"How about a compromise? You get in the car, I'll drive you to your house in Hollywood, and I can tell you all about it on the way. We'll have plenty of time to talk in the car. It's almost a two-hour drive to Hollywood from here." Sharla opened the car door.

"I just don't know. I mean, you're not going to stick me with that needle again, are you?"

"No! That's for Jane, when she gets off her medication. I would never use it on you."

"You did use it on me!" Leeza shouted.

"That's because I thought you were Jane!"

"Do you have it with you?"

"Of course! When Sylvia called me and told me what was going on at her house, I thought Jane was going off again, so, I brought it with me."

"Why does she keep your mom so doped up?"

"I'll tell you all about it, if you just get in the car." Sharla held out her hand in invitation.

"Why do you care if I get in the car? Just let me go. Someone else can give me a ride home."

"If your driver brought you here, why can't he come and get you?"

"He doesn't know I'm here. I mean, he thinks Jane's me."

"So, you think Jane has him fooled, like you had me fooled?"

"Yeah. It would be pretty easy for her, because I'm so changeable, he wouldn't think anything of her, no matter how eccentric she is acting."

"If she has been there all this time without her medication, there's no telling how she is acting."

"Why is she on medication, anyway? What is the matter with her?"

"Let's get in the car, and I'll explain everything."

"Why can't you just tell me? Why do I have to get in the car?"

"I want to know where Jane is! Can't you see, we have to go get her so I can bring her home! She can become dangerous if she is not on her medication! So, let's get in the car, I'll take you home, to your house in Hollywood, and then I'll bring Jane back home, to our house, with me."

Sharla was making sense, but Leeza was afraid to trust her. What if she were just trying to trick her into getting in the car so she could drug her again? Leeza considered the alternative. She could start walking down the highway and hope to get a ride from a stranger, and then hope that stranger would take her to her house. That seemed even more risky right now. She had no choice but to trust Sharla on this one.

"Okay, let's go," Leeza finally agreed. She approached the car slowly, watching Sharla closely.

"Great! Hey, can I come inside your house? It must be fabulous," Sharla said, as she got in the driver's seat. "If it's not too much trouble, maybe you can give me a tour? I have never been in a mansion before."

Leeza relaxed a little and got in on the passenger side. Sharla must have read about her house in those magazines. "It would be my pleasure," she said, then she asked, "Hey, where's Shari?"

"She's still at the babysitter. When Sylvia called me, I was at work, so I just came straight here without picking her up."

"How did you know I – or Jane – would come here?"

"Sylvia saw you go down on the beach, and I figured, if you were trying to go south, you would have to end up here." Sharla started the car and got on the highway going south.

"So, what's the deal with Jane?" Leeza asked.

"Well, she had a breakdown a couple of years ago, or, actually, about eighteen months ago."

"A breakdown?"

"Yeah, so now she needs to be on medication."

"That's it?" Leeza looked at Sharla, wanting to know more.

"That's it."

"You said it was a long story."

"Well..." Sharla appeared to concentrate on her driving.

"So what about your mom? What was she talking about?"

"She was talking to you?"

"Yeah, she said all kinds of crazy things."

"My mother is not crazy!"

"No, I didn't mean that she is crazy, but I couldn't make sense of what she was saying." Leeza looked straight ahead at the road.

"What was she saying?"

"Well, she was saying you are a good girl and you wouldn't kill anyone." Leeza turned just her eyes to see Sharla's reaction.

"That's not crazy. That's true. I mean, I wouldn't kill anyone."

"Are you a good girl?"

"My mom thinks so." Sharla smiled slightly.

"But are you?"

"Yeah. I'm pretty good."

"Yeah? Nobody's that good." Leeza knew how people were; she knew human nature, and people were generally not good.

"What else did my mom say?"

Leeza checked on the scenery, to be sure they were continuing in the correct direction. So far, Sharla was being true to her word. They were still going south.

"She kept saying I wasn't her daughter."

"You're not."

"I know, but how did she know I wasn't Jane?"

"A mother always knows her own daughters."

"Speaking of daughters, why did Jane tell me Shari is *her* daughter?"

"Jane said that?" Sharla's eyes widened.

"Yeah. Shari is your daughter, isn't she?"

"Yes, she is."

"So, do you have a boyfriend?"

"That's none of your business." Sharla pursed her lips tightly.

"You have a baby!"

"My private life is not your business."

"Sorry! You don't have to get all in a huff! Does Jane have a boyfriend?"

"Do you?"

"Of course! My life is no secret! Everyone knows that Chad Manager is my boyfriend!"

"Chad Manager?" Sharla laughed.

"You know, Chad Manager, the model? His face is everywhere! He's in every magazine, and he's on TV all the time. And his body, too, he just did that commercial for those swimsuits."

"Oh, yeah, of course," Sharla said knowingly. "Chad Manager is your boyfriend."

"Jane told me she has a boyfriend."

"Hmmm... did she tell you his name?"

"Yeah, but I don't remember what she said."

"Did she say I had a boyfriend?"

"No, she didn't mention it. Do you?"

"Not your business," Sharla snapped.

"Look, I'm not going to tell anyone. Your love life, or lack of, doesn't matter to me, anyway. If you don't have a boyfriend, who is your baby's father?"

"I told you, it's none of your business!"

"Okay, okay! Take it easy! Maybe you need a little of that medication. According to Sylvia, anyone who gets upset should take some medication," Leeza snorted.

"Just leave Sylvia out of this. She has enough to deal with, taking care of Mom and all. If it weren't for Sylvia taking care of Mom, she would have to be in a nursing home."

"Really? But she doesn't look that old."

"No, it's not because of her age. She's only 42. But because of her breakdown, she has to have full-time care."

"So both your mom and your sister had breakdowns? How unlikely is that?" Leeza threw up her hands.

"Wellllll.......... we found out after Mom's breakdown that she was mentally unstable, so it's possible that Jane inherited some of those characteristics, or, um, her mental instability."

"So it was mental instability that caused them both to have breakdowns? I mean, did they both have them at the same time? No, that wouldn't be possible, would it? Which one, I mean, I, um, am I getting too personal? I'm just curious."

"Hey, this is the Hollywood highway coming up. Should I go this way?" Sharla asked.

"Yeah, just get us into Hollywood, and I can find my house."

"What street is it on?"

"I'm not sure."

"You don't know what street you live on?"

"I told you, I never bother with the details. Someone else takes care of all that."

"Oh, great, so I'm going to just be driving up and down every street in Hollywood until we find your house. Great. I should have brought Shari with us, because this could take days."

"It won't take that long! Once we get into Hollywood, I'll be able to tell you how to get to my house."

"I've been to Hollywood before, and it's not a little place. We could really get lost in there."

"I know, but I know my way around, once we get there. We'll find it in no time."

"I doubt it." Sharla shook her head. "We'll see."

"We will! So, are you going to tell me what happened to Jane? I mean, did she just have a breakdown for no reason, or what?" She wanted Sharla to tell her what really happened.

Sharla didn't say anything.

"Burton!" Leeza suddenly remembered.

"What?" Sharla shrieked.

"Burton! Jane said her boyfriend's name is Burton."

"It's not Burton!"

CHAPTER 32

"That's what she told me."

"No, that's not possible." Sharla shook her head violently.

"Do you know anyone named Burton?"

"No, we don't know anyone by that name," Sharla insisted.

"So why would she say that's her boyfriend's name?"

"I don't know! She shouldn't have said that!" she shouted.

"Well, she did."

"Just forget it, okay?"

"It's forgotten. Man, what is it with that name? Is it going to cause you to have a breakdown, too?"

"I said, just drop it! Don't mention that name, ever again!"

"Okay, okay! It's dropped! Hey, don't you have to turn up there? You need to get in the other lane."

"Yeah, I am," Sharla said, working her way to the right lane so she could take the Hollywood exit.

"Yes! Hollywood, coming right up! We're going to be there in no time, no time at all."

"So, it's this first exit?"

"Yeah, this is the one, right up here."

Sharla turned onto the exit. "So, left or right?"

"Go left at this corner," Leeza said. Things looked slightly familiar. After they turned, she said, "Take a right at the next corner, and then follow that street for awhile."

"You're sure this is the way?"

"Sure, I'm sure! I know the way to my own house, I just don't know the street names. I'll know it when I see it. The street is lined with palm trees, and all the houses have big yards and hedges so you can't really see the houses from the street, but the houses are really big."

"They are all mansions, aren't they?"

"Yeah, how do you know?"

"You said that earlier."

"I did?"

"Yeah, don't you remember? You were talking about your mansion, on a street full of mansions?"

"I don't remember saying that, but that's what it is." She was really getting excited, finally being so close to home. She could use some pampering from her staff right about now: a full-body massage, a nice, fresh meal, maybe a leisurely swim in her pool.

"Hey, do you want to go swimming when we get there?" she asked.

"I don't think so," Sharla said.

"I have a really nice pool."

"I don't have my swimming suit with me."

"You can use one of mine. I have all kinds of them in the pool cabana."

"Pool cabana? No, I don't think so."

"Well, it's really private. You don't need a swimming suit."

"No, I need a swimming suit, but I just don't feel like swimming. I need to get Jane and take her home. Who knows what condition she might be in? Without having her medication for a few days, she could really be freaking out."

"She's probably just having such a great time, she doesn't want to leave." Leeza smiled at the image of Jane in her life.

"Yeah, right."

"Well, you haven't seen anything about Leeza Hamilton on the news lately, have you? I mean, if she had a breakdown and they took her to a hospital or something, don't you think it would be all over the TV by now?"

"Oh, yes, everything that Leeza Hamilton does is always news," Sharla agreed, nodding.

"That's what I'm saying. So she must be all right, if she hasn't been in the news."

"Wouldn't that be weird if she wrote a new song or something, and then Leeza Hamilton made it famous, saying she wrote it?"

"That couldn't happen!" Leeza insisted.

"No, I'm just saying, what if."

"No! Leeza never sings another person's songs."

"But nobody would know! Everyone would think she is you, Leeza."

"That won't happen, believe me."

Sharla stopped the car. "Okay, left or right? Which way to your house?"

They were at a stop sign. Leeza looked both ways, but neither one seemed to be the right way. Had they missed a turn?

"Go left," she said. They had to be getting close.

Sharla turned left and Leeza looked at the houses on this street. They were away from the downtown area, but these houses weren't big enough to be in Leeza's neighborhood.

"Take a right at that corner," she said, looking for any landmark that might tell her they were going in the right direction. "Okay, turn up here, go left."

They drove up one street and down the next, up and down, up and down, until they had covered the side of the hill. Leeza was getting impatient: where was her street? They were so close, but they just couldn't find the right street! Sharla was strangely calm, following Leeza's directions with an unusual amount of patience.

"Why don't you call your house and get directions?" Sharla finally asked, after nearly an hour of searching.

"I don't have my cell phone," Leeza said.

"You can use mine," Sharla offered.

"I don't know the number," Leeza confessed.

"You don't know your own phone number?"

"Who does these days? Everything is in speed dial."

"I have speed dial, but I still know the important phone numbers."

"Well, like I said, I'm not a detail person."

"I think you are."

"What do you mean by that?" Leeza turned to look at Sharla.

"Nothing. Let's just find your house. Which way now?"

They were at another stop sign, and still, although this area seemed familiar, this was not her street.

"Go left," she said, looking down the street.

"We already went that way. Maybe we could get a map."

"How would that help, if I don't know the name of the street?"

"I know! We could get one of those maps of the stars' homes!"

"No, my house is not on that tour."

"Really? Why not?"

"Well, you can't see it from the street, so what would be the use? A busload of people driving up to see a huge hedge?"

"Some people might like that. I mean, they would be on your street just hopeful for a glimpse of your limousine coming out of the driveway."

"Yeah, well, it's not."

They drove around Hollywood for another forty-five minutes, with Leeza directing Sharla to go up and down each street on the grid. Finally, Sharla drove down the hill and pulled into a gas station.

"I'm going to get some gas," she said. "Maybe while I'm in there, I'll ask if anyone knows where Leeza Hamilton lives. I mean, if we are in your neighborhood, maybe someone knows where you live."

"Yeah, sure, give it a try," Leeza said, frustrated. They were so close, but where was it? Where was her house? They had driven by large and small houses, and the neighborhoods were almost like hers, but they just couldn't find it. She searched for a clue, any clue as to how to get home, but she didn't see anything that would guide her to her home.

Sharla came out of the mini-mart and pumped the gas. When she finished, she cleaned the windshield and then got back into the car.

"No one in there knows where you live," she said.

"Maybe we could just go back that way, over there," Leeza suggested.

"I don't think it's anywhere near here," Sharla said.

"Why do you say that?"

"Well, one guy in there knows where all the stars live in this area, and he said Leeza Hamilton doesn't live around here. He would know. He gave me a list of famous people that live right in this neighborhood. Did you know we drove right past Tyler Ball's house?"

"Really?"

"Yeah, it's that big yellow house, right up there. You can see it from here. Right back there is where Sierra Daly lives, and across the way, Roxanne Fields owns that big brick house with all those evergreen trees."

Leeza didn't recall that she lived anywhere near Tyler Ball or Roxanne Fields. She didn't even know Sierra Daly lived in Hollywood. "Let's go back to the other side of Hollywood."

"We already covered that area. Maybe you live near Hollywood, but not quite in Hollywood?"

"No! My house is in Hollywood!"

"I bought this map," Sharla said, pulling a map of Hollywood and a pen out of her purse. "Okay, these are the streets we have covered." She traced their route into the city, and she colored all the streets they had already checked.

"Let me see that," Leeza said, when Sharla had finished. She searched for a street name that would trigger her memory, but she couldn't find anything that could tell her where she lived.

"Do you live on a hill?" Sharla asked. "Maybe you're on the outskirts, like up here, or somewhere like that."

"No! The street is…" Leeza couldn't remember.

"We have driven on every street in every residential neighborhood," Sharla said.

"We must have missed one, because we didn't go on my street."

"I really need to get my sister and bring her home," Sharla said.

"I know! But I just don't know!"

"Just tell me which way to go."

"I don't know! Just drive!" Leeza threw up her hands in frustration.

"I have to have some sort of direction. I know, let's go up this hill, and we'll check that area, right there on the map. We haven't been up there yet."

That had to be the area where she lived. It was the only one left that they had not yet seen. "Okay, let's go," Leeza said.

Sharla drove up the hill and arrived in an area that was cut off from the rest of Hollywood by a gate.

"Do you have a key?" Sharla asked, looking at the gate. "Or a key code?"

"No, it's not in here," Leeza said, disappointed. "It must be somewhere else."

Sharla drove down the hill and turned a corner.

"We've already been on this street," Leeza said.

"I know. I'm just going to go this way. Maybe you'll see something you recognize."

Leeza watched out the window, silently cursing herself for not paying more attention to important details, like where she lived; specifically, the name of her own street. They had to find it!

CHAPTER 33

Sharla pulled the car to the side of the road and stopped. She opened the map and looked at it for a few minutes. She handed the map to Leeza.

"We have gone on every street in this entire area. There is no other street for us to check. Where is your house, Leeza?"

Leeza looked at the map, trying to make sense of it. She looked at the streets Sharla had colored, which were all the streets in this area, but she didn't really know how to read a map. They must have missed a street somewhere! She looked for a familiar street name. "What about over here?" she asked, pointing to an area on the map.

"We went there," Sharla said.

"How about here?"

"We already went there, too."

"How about right here? We didn't go here."

"No, that is going out of the residential area. That's where there are some apartments, but there aren't any houses there, or any mansions." Sharla sighed loudly.

"What about over in this part?"

"That's not in Hollywood, look. See? Do you live in West Hollywood? Or Beverly Hills?"

"No! It's in Hollywood! What about up on that hill?"

"We looked there."

"Did we go over there?" Leeza pointed to a huge general area.

"Yes! We went everywhere on this map!"

"You're saying we covered all these streets already?"

"Yes, we went on every one of them." Sharla nodded.

"Over here?"

"That's not a residential area. That's where we came in, remember? There are no mansions in that area."

Leeza studied the map. Her house had to be here somewhere! Why couldn't she think of the street name?

"Well, I hate to say this, but your house is not in Hollywood."

"Yes, it is!" Leeza insisted.

"Just listen to me for a minute!"

"Okay, but it IS in Hollywood."

"I need to go back home, and I need to take Jane with me."

"How can you take her home if we can't find my house?"

Sharla started the car.

"Do you know where she is?" Leeza asked.

"I think so."

"How do you know? Did she call you?"

Sharla began to drive. Somewhat encouraged, Leeza looked out the window for any landmark that might show her they were on their way to her house. Sharla drove up a big hill that looked familiar to Leeza. Maybe she did know where to go!

They went across a ridge and then down another hill. Sharla kept driving, right out of Hollywood, and she got on the highway going north.

"Where are you going?"

"I'm taking Jane home."

"Where is she?"

"I'm taking her home."

"What are you talking about?"

Sharla took the next exit, pulled into a parking lot and stopped the car. She turned off the engine.

Leeza quickly scanned the area. "What are you doing? Is Jane here? Why are you stopping here?"

Sharla took off her seat belt and looked at Leeza.

"You are Jane," she said softly.

"No, I'm not! I am Leeza! I'm Leeza Hamilton!"

"You think you are Leeza Hamilton, but you are really my sister, Jane."

"I AM Leeza Hamilton! I live in Hollywood, and I need to get back home!"

"No, you are my sister. You had a breakdown."

"I did not! You have me mistaken for your sister, but I'm not your sister!" Leeza tried to open the car door, but it wouldn't open. "Let me out of here!"

"Just listen to me for a minute," Sharla said.

"You have one minute," Leeza warned.

"That's all I need," she said calmly. "You are my sister, Jane, and you had a breakdown. You have multiple personalities, and one of them apparently is Leeza Hamilton. You need to come home with me so I can take care of you."

"I need to go to my own house!"

"Where is your house?"

"I don't know!"

"It's because you don't have a house. I wanted to prove that to you, so you can understand what I am about to tell you."

"What are you talking about?"

"I'm going to attempt to explain everything to you."

"Explain what?"

"I think it's time you knew the truth."

"The truth? The truth about what? What are you talking about?"

"You had a breakdown when you killed Daddy. Ever since that day, you have struggled with who you are. Sometimes you are Jane, but you can't remember what happened that day, and sometimes you are someone else, with a whole different life of your own. You always have an elaborate history and background concocted, but there are always missing pieces, like today. You are not the famous Leeza Hamilton. You are just my sister, Jane.

"Then Mom had a breakdown when she found out you killed Daddy. She freaked out and she hasn't been the same since. She disowned you that day, that's why she says you are not her daughter. But you ARE her daughter. She just can't accept what you did."

The scenes of the incident flashed through Leeza's mind, as she remembered watching the movie about this crime. As she recalled the red splotches, she felt physical pain. She blinked her eyes to erase the memory. It didn't happen to her! She didn't do it! That was not her life! That was just a movie she saw! She was not Jane!

"It doesn't make sense," Leeza said. "If I killed someone, wouldn't I be in jail?"

"You were only 17, and there were extenuating circumstances."

"So when did this happen? I'm 26 now. You're trying to tell me, I've been crazy for almost 10 years, living some kind of weird double life?"

"No, you are only 19. This happened less than two years ago."

"I am not your sister! I have been famous since I was a teenager! Wait, she's only 19? Wow, she looks so much older than that. Hey, don't try to confuse me! My name is Leeza Hamilton! I am a performer, and I live in a mansion in Hollywood! I have a boyfriend named Chad, and he's probably really worried about me by now!"

"I am sure of that," Sharla said.

"So just take me back to Hollywood and let me off somewhere. I'll find my own way home."

"I can't leave you here. I am responsible for you."

"Why in the world would you be responsible for me?"

"Because you saved my life!"

CHAPTER 34

"I saved your life." Leeza stared at Sharla.

"Yes, you did."

"How did I save your life? Or, I should ask, how did Jane save your life?"

Sharla looked out the window, reluctant to answer the question.

"If I saved your life, I would remember it. I haven't ever saved anyone's life. I don't save anything, I just live, and other people take care of my needs."

"I take care of you."

"No, I have a driver named Dennis, and a cook named Hans, and a personal trainer named Gretchen, and I have two personal assistants, Nita and Karman. Plus, I have a gardener named Dodge Dishman and he is also Karman's boyfriend. Plus, I have several other people on my staff, that I support."

"I am the one who does all those things for you," Sharla said softly.

"No, you don't! I didn't even know you until a few days ago, when I traded places with Jane!"

"Don't you think it's weird, you and Jane look so much alike? It's because you share the same body! That's why we can't find her!"

"We can't find her because we can't find my house!"

"No, you are her! You are Jane! You have to realize that and pull yourself together!"

"No, I am not Jane! I am Leeza!"

"Your doctor told me not to do this, but I am getting sick and tired of you just going off into your own world, and acting like you don't have to do anything! You used to be the responsible one! You used to take care of everything! You used to be aware and concerned about everything we were doing! Now you just pretend to be someone else when you don't want to be accountable for your actions! You just let me do everything!"

"Hey! You are talking to me like you really think I am Jane! I'm not Jane! I am Leeza Hamilton! You can't talk to me like that!"

"No, you just think you are Leeza Hamilton! That is another one of your personalities!"

"Wait a minute. You are saying, because Jane killed your father, she, all of a sudden, became a split personality?"

"Maybe I shouldn't have brought this up to you, but I'm just trying to make you face the facts! You are Jane! Jane is you! I'm trying to force you to see, you just made up the life of Leeza!"

"No, you are wrong! I'm not Jane! And how could I be, if she's only 19? I have been living in Hollywood ever since I left home, almost 10 years ago!"

"When you were 17, right?"

"That's right!"

"So why did you leave home?"

"To become somebody!"

"And your parents were okay with that, you leaving home and all?"

"My father died, and my mother and I had a disagreement, so I ran away."

"That's exactly what happened to Jane. Our father died, and she and my mom had a disagreement, so Jane ran away – but she couldn't physically escape, so she escaped into her own mind; your own mind. That is exactly what the doctor said."

"I have never been to a shrink in my life!"

"No, Leeza hasn't, but Jane has."

"Well, okay, then, Jane has. But I AM NOT JANE!" Leeza wanted desperately to get out of the car, but she couldn't. She was trapped here, with Sharla. She just wanted to go home.

"Look, all I want to do is go home."

"And I'm going to take you home."

"I don't want to go back to your home! I want to go to my own home, in Hollywood! We are right here! Just go back down the highway and drop me off in Hollywood. I'll find my own way home, and when I do, I'll call you and let you know where you can pick up Jane."

"I can't do that. It would be too dangerous for you. I can't let you out of my sight down here. It's bad enough that you escaped from our house."

"It's *your* house! It's not my house! My house is in Hollywood!"

"We have been over this too many times. We have to go back home now."

"Just let me get out here and I'll walk."

"I told you, I can't leave you here. You have to come home with me, right now."

Leeza was really frustrated. She couldn't go back to Jane's house. She tried to think of a way to escape.

"I need to go to the bathroom," she said.

"Well, so do I, but we're not getting out of the car here. You are too fast for me, and I can't let you get away from me again. We'll go to that rest area up ahead, the one that has the armed guards." Sharla started the car and began driving again. She pulled onto the freeway going north.

Leeza sat back in the seat, frantic to find a way to escape while they were still somewhat in the vicinity of her house.

"So, Leeza, if you are 26, what did you do last year, for your 25th birthday? A big star like you must have had a huge celebration."

"Yes, of course! Hans fixed a wonderful meal, and, actually, Chad threw a surprise party for me. Everyone who is anyone was there, including the press. You probably read about it in all the magazines."

"I must have missed it."

"Don't you go into supermarkets? It was on the cover at all the newsstands. You must have seen it."

"I didn't see it – because it didn't exist! You are making all this up!"

"No, I'm not! I am not your sister! I think you are the crazy one! You can't even tell the difference between a real star and your own sister, a Plain Jane!"

"Okay, I'm going to try another approach. I will make you remember what happened, why you split yourself up."

"Make me remember? How are you going to do that? You can't make me remember something I didn't do."

"Oh, but you did do it, and you are going to remember."

"Uh, if it's so traumatic that it made your sister have split personalities, then do you think it's a good idea to remind her? I mean, if I were her, which I'm NOT, should you be doing this? Well, go ahead, because it's not going to hurt me. I wasn't there."

"No, but Jane was."

"My point exactly!"

"You can stop me any time, as soon as you start to remember."

"You can be sure, if I start to remember, I will let you know. But still, it's impossible, because you've got the wrong person! You should be telling Jane this!"

"I am telling Jane, if you'll just listen."

"You really must be crazy."

CHAPTER 35

Sharla continued driving, staring straight ahead while she began to tell the story.

"We lived in the old Waverly house, across town. You know, the big, old, blue house with white trim, the one that sits about halfway up the big hill. It's not on the beach, but because it's so high on the hill, you can see the beach from there. Anyway, we lived there, the four of us, Mom and Daddy and you and me."

Leeza tried to picture in her mind the house that Sharla was describing, but she hadn't seen it. So far, nothing she said was familiar to her.

"Most of the rooms we used were on the main floor. On the second floor, the rooms were all filled with furniture and stuff the Waverlys were storing. They went overseas, remember? We were really just house-sitting for them because Daddy lost his job, so Mom went to work part-time at Flipman's. You really wanted one of the bedrooms upstairs because it had a window seat, so we cleaned up that room for you to use. You painted it yourself, lavender, remember?"

Leeza shook her head. This began to sound a little like the movie she had seen about the girl who killed her father.

"My room was downstairs, across from the den. Mom and Daddy had the room at the back of the house, closest to the kitchen. Daddy cooked for us since Mom was working, and you and I took turns cleaning the kitchen. Mom was always really tired.

"One day Daddy told me to go to the store and get some onions, but I didn't want to go because I was trying to finish my homework. He got really mad at me, so I ran upstairs to ask you to go instead of me. You wanted to get out of the house, so you agreed to go. I stayed up in your room so Daddy wouldn't see me, so he wouldn't know I disobeyed him." Sharla's voice began to tremble, and Leeza noticed a tear was running down her cheek.

"Daddy came upstairs. I could hear him, and I was scared, so I hid from him. I don't know how he knew where I was, but he found me and he started hitting me, beating me, yelling at me that he would teach me to obey him. He ripped my clothes and he started to really hurt me. He made me bleed, and I was afraid to cry, but he hurt me so much."

Leeza now felt as if she were watching the movie again as Sharla told the story: up the stairs, into the room, the blood all over the place, the man hurting the girl, the fireplace poker hitting him in the head.

"I just wanted him to stop hurting me, and I screamed. I thought he was going to kill me. Then I saw you there, behind him, and all of a sudden, he stopped moving, he stopped hurting me, and he fell on me. I saw blood was splattered everywhere, and you had something in your hand. You yelled that you weren't going to let him hurt me like he hurt you. Do you remember, Jane? Do you remember how he hurt you? You saved my life. Do you remember?"

"How could I remember? I am not Jane!" Leeza shouted.

"But you are Jane. You have to remember.

"You ran away from the house and you left me there. I didn't know what to do. I went downstairs, and I tried to clean myself up. I knew he was dead, but I couldn't go back upstairs and look at him. Then Mom came home and she freaked out when she saw the blood everywhere. When I told her what Daddy did to me and what you did to him, and how you saved my life, she started yelling and screaming and saying it wasn't his fault, and we should be good girls so this wouldn't happen. She kept trying to wake him up, and she wouldn't listen to me. I called the police and they came to the house. She tried to act like nothing was out of the ordinary, but it was obvious that she was lying because there was blood everywhere. They followed the trail up the steps and they found his body. Mom and I were in the kitchen, and the policewoman wanted me to sit down, but I couldn't because I was in too much pain. She asked me to tell her what happened, and I told her Daddy raped me. Mom slapped my face, and then she snapped. Her eyes got a stare in them and she couldn't see me or hear me anymore.

"When the police found you, you said you were Mildred LeBoo. You had blood all over you, but you couldn't remember anything about what just happened. When they examined you and me and Mom and the crime scene, they decided not to press charges against you. You and Mom went into a mental hospital for a while, not together, I mean, in separate areas, then they released you into my custody after I turned 18. You have displayed two or three different personalities to me, and just recently, you became Jane again, but you haven't had any memory of the incident."

"No," Leeza said, shaking her head. This wasn't possible. She didn't have anything to do with this. They had to find Jane so she could prove that she, Leeza, hadn't been involved, that she wasn't there, that she had been living her own life for the past 26 years.

"Yes," Sharla said, wiping her tears. "You have added lives and years of your own, in your own mind, but you are my sister, Jane."

Leeza could not accept this. She was a famous performer, and she needed to get back home so she could get ready for her next performance. All of this was too far-fetched. How dare Sharla insist that she, the famous Leeza Hamilton, was really just a Plain Jane with multiple personalities?

"You are mistaken. If all this did happen, I didn't have anything to do with it. Like I said, I am not your sister."

"Come on! Come back, Jane! I know you're in there!"

"Hey! Pay attention to the road!" Leeza said, as they swerved into another lane.

"What do you mean, if all this did happen? Are you saying that I made it up?"

"No, I'm not saying that, but–"

"You want proof? You want proof?" Sharla was really raising her voice.

"Proof?"

"Shari! Nine months later, Shari was born!"

"What? What kind of proof is that?"

"Her father is Burton! Our father, Burton, is Shari's father!"

"Come on, let me out. Here. Now. You are sick! You have to let me out of here."

"You can't run away from your own life!"

"This is not my life! I have my own life, and this is not it!"

"Jane! Snap out of it! You were doing so well! You were getting so close!"

"I told you, I am not Jane! My name is Leeza Hamilton, and I demand that you take me back to Hollywood, right now! Let me out of this car! You are crazy!"

"I am your sister! Who else knows you like I know you?"

"You don't know me! You know someone else! You know Jane! You better stop this car right now, or I am going to turn you in!"

"Who is going to believe you?"

"At least I am sane! You are crazy! All they have to do is look at me and they will know who I am! Everybody knows me!"

Leeza reached over to grab the steering wheel. She had to stop this car! They swerved to the right and Sharla regained control of the car. Then, in one swift movement, Leeza saw a flash of silver as she realized, too late, that Sharla was sticking her with a needle.

"It's not sterilized!" she attempted to shout, just as she was losing consciousness.

CHAPTER 36

Soft clouds surrounded her as she awakened in a warm place. Where was she? She was in some sort of white room... a hospital room? She tried to move, but her muscles did not respond to the signals she was sending to them. Maybe she was outside of her body, in heaven. She couldn't think of where she had been or who she was. She saw faces without mouths, beings communicating without speaking, hovering above her, about her, through her. She could understand them as if they were part of her. She was so comfortable here, so at ease... until words intruded into this world, tumbling into her sense of awareness, drawing her to another place.

She felt herself being pulled at an extremely fast pace through a long tunnel, zooming, zooming, through a small hole in the wall to return to her own body again.

These are words, and these are people talking, speaking, using their mouths, she thought. Her vision was blurry, but she knew she was in a room with other people, and she was a person. Nothing made any sense, but everything was so logical. She had been gone, and now she had returned.

"It's okay," she said, pleased that her mouth was working so well.

The movement around her stopped and huge faces peered into her eyes.

"She's awake," a voice said, as if it were coming from under water.

"Did she speak?" another voice said. That one must have been the voice of a laughing hyena.

She began to laugh and laugh. They were so funny! They had come to entertain her!

"She's pulling through," the under-water voice bubbled.

She couldn't stop laughing! Her own personal comedy team was right here, with her! They cared about her, enough to come to her rescue, right in this very room!

She laughed herself to sleep. As she was leaving the room, she saw herself going over a waterfall and then swimming, swimming, in the ocean, on the way to the South Pole. She greeted swimming penguins with a high-five, slapping their lifted wings with her open palm. The creatures were so friendly to her, she kept smiling as she swam, skimming over the top of the water. She saw an eagle swoop over the water, and she bowed her head in reverence, honored that he had chosen to fly over her.

She opened her eyes and she was in a different room, a familiar room. Somebody was looking right at her face – she knew this person. This was her sister... no, she thought she was her sister, but she wasn't really her sister. Beside her stood herself, looking down at her. She tried to make sense of this grouping of people, but the meaning temporarily escaped her. No, wait, these were sisters... Sharla and Jane were both looking at her.

CHAPTER 37

Leeza felt a huge wave of relief wash over her. Now the truth was evident!

"I'm glad Jane came back," she managed to say.

"So am I," Sharla said, smiling at her. "You have been gone for a long time."

"I can't... I don't..." she began. She wasn't sure what she was trying to say.

"Shhh... you don't need to talk right now. There will be time enough for that later," Sharla said.

"When...?" she didn't know how to finish the sentence.

"We are hoping you can get out of bed today, but if you don't feel up to it, you can keep resting," Sharla said. "There is no need for you to hurry."

"Hurry," she repeated. She did have a reason to hurry, but she didn't fully comprehend it.

"I'll be right back," Sharla said. "You just relax." She left the room.

Jane held up a newspaper for Sharla to see. The headline read 'Singer/Performer Leeza Hamilton – Missing!' The subheading stated that she had missed her concert and couldn't be found.

"Oh, no!" she said, struggling to sit. She recognized it now; she was in Jane's room, and she had missed her performance! Well, now that Sharla knew that she wasn't Jane, she would help her return to her own home and they could get this whole mess back in order. She didn't like to have anything out of order.

"What's the matter?" Sharla said, rushing back into the room.

"The performance," was all she could say.

"Yes, it was quite a performance, I will grant you that," Sharla said.

"No!" she shouted.

"You need to calm yourself," Sharla said soothingly. "Doc Munsinger is getting your dosages corrected. That last time, it was a little too much."

"Do-si-do?" What did she mean?

"You must be hungry," Sharla said. "You haven't eaten in quite some time."

"Home," she said. The sentences weren't where they should be; only a few words could be delivered at this time.

"Yes, yes, isn't it wonderful?"

Jane stood behind her sister, nodding her head and smiling. Everybody was happy that each was going to be in her own home. Maybe Jane had her cell phone! She could call Dennis to come and get her and take her back to her own house!

"I'll go and make you a sandwich," Sharla said. "How about turkey and cheese? Mmmm, doesn't that sound good? And we have some potato chips to go with it. Or do you want a bowl of soup? We have a can of your favorite, bean with bacon."

She didn't want soup from a can. She wanted something fresh, made by Hans. She didn't eat potato chips: they were too salty for her taste. The only bread she liked to eat was the fresh bread Hans made for her, 100% whole wheat. All these thoughts were going through her mind and she was trying to formulate a sentence, but Sharla left the room before any of the words could make it to her mouth.

Jane smiled at her. She must be happy to be home again, with her sister, and in her own home. Leeza wanted to talk to her about her adventures in Hollywood, at her house, but the thoughts were flying too fast for the mouth to catch them. Jane stepped into her closet and pulled out the red cloak: the red cloak that had started this whole ordeal; the red cloak that had nearly ruined her life.

She watched her suspiciously as Jane put on the cloak. Without a word, she slipped out of the room and sneaked down the steps.

She had to stop her! Jane was going to go back to her life and leave her here! With great effort, she fought her way out of the covers on the bed. She stood and her legs melted beneath her.

CHAPTER 38

Sharla ran into the room. "What happened? What are you trying to do? Here, let me help you."

"Stop her!"

"What?"

"Stop Jane!"

"What are you talking about?"

"Jane! The red cloak!"

"You need to get back into bed. I'll call Doc Munsinger to come. Honestly, I don't know what to do with you any more."

"Let me go home."

"Jane, you are home."

"Jane just left!"

"Oh, dear, who are you now?"

"No! I am never Jane! I have never been Jane! Jane just escaped in the red cloak!"

"I thought you were back," Sharla said, disappointed. "I thought when I told you what happened, you would remember. You were back, for a while."

"Why don't you believe me?"

"Because I know you. I know who you are. I want my sister back. I was just hoping... they told me not to get my hopes up, but I thought I could fix things if you just remembered the truth."

"Go get her!" Leeza pointed at the door.

"Who?"

"Jane! She just left! She's wearing the red cloak!"

Sharla looked in the closet. "Where is it?"

"I told you, Jane is wearing it! She just left! You can still catch her, if you go now!"

"I am not going to leave you alone. You are Jane. I am staying here until the doctor arrives."

"Please, let me go home." She was so tired, tired of fighting, tired of arguing, tired of trying to make Sharla understand and know who she really was.

"You are home," Sharla said, trying to calm her. "You are here, at home, with your sister, and your baby niece is in the next room asleep. Now, just relax, and the doctor will be here soon."

Leeza wanted to cry, but she had no tears.

"This isn't my home," she whispered.

Now Sharla started to cry. "I don't want to let them take you away," she sobbed. "As long as you are threatening to leave, they want to take you and lock you up. Please, can you just act like you are happy here? Can you just fake it, while they come to evaluate you? I don't want them to take you away, but really, I am just so tired, and I am just one person... I can't do it all any more."

"Don't cry," Leeza whispered. She could not let them take her to some hospital where she would be locked in a room. "I'll behave," she promised.

She closed her eyes in preparation for her evaluation. They could be here any minute. She took a deep breath in order to relax. She would pretend to be Jane and she would cooperate with them while they did their tests. Then she would have a chance to escape and go home later, when they stopped watching her. She would catch Jane and then she would return to her own life.

CHAPTER 39

"Wake up, Leeza!" Nita said, gently patting her face. "It's almost time for you to go on stage!"

Leeza opened her eyes and smiled. *This* was her real life.

www.ingramcontent.com/pod-product-compliance
Lightning Source LLC
Chambersburg PA
CBHW070937130626
46555CB00001B/470